CAUGHT IN A SPIDER'S WEB

A Cozy Quilts Club Mystery
Book 4

MARSHA DEFILIPPO

To get the latest information on new releases, excerpts and more, be sure to sign up for Marsha's newsletter.

https://marshadefilippo.com/newsletter

Dedicated to
The Cotton Cupboard Quilt Shop
Bangor, Maine

They have all the quilting essentials.

Chapter 1

Sarah Pascal hummed along with the tune playing in her head as she studied the document on her computer screen. She was still in her sweats and planned to stay that way for the rest of the day. It was one of the perks of working from home as a cyber security analyst that she took advantage of from time to time. Her golden retriever, Max, was curled up on his dog bed strategically placed to soak up the heat from the sun coming in through the window. It was a cozy counterpoint to the late October shift in temperatures outside. His gentle snores were adding to the sense of domestic bliss Sarah was feeling today.

Her wife, Ashley, was out of town for business and wouldn't be back until later that day. Ashley's job as a district manager for a retail drugstore chain sometimes required her to travel to the northern part of the state. That meant an overnight stay because of the distances involved traveling back and forth from Bangor.

Sarah's stomach growled, distracting her from the notes she was typing for the document analysis. Just one more notation, though, and she would be finished.

A smile crossed her face as she gazed down at Max. He was only three months old when she and Ashley brought him home from the animal shelter during one of their volunteer stints for an adopt-a-thon event. He'd first been rescued from a puppy mill and then again when they adopted him. He was scrawny and shivering with fright when Sarah picked him up and held him close to her chest, but their eyes connected, and he cautiously licked her chin. That had sealed the deal. Adopting a dog hadn't been on their agenda, but they signed the adoption papers and brought him home that same day. *You're a long way from that little ball of fur, aren't you boy?*

It was their love of dogs and cats that had been the first spark of attraction for her and Ashley. They'd met as volunteers at an event for the local animal shelter over a decade ago and hit it off immediately. As time went on, they discovered other common interests beyond their passion for volunteering and animals and their relationship blossomed. Their commitment to each other was based on mutual respect and understanding of the values and life aspirations that mattered to them both.

"What do you think, buddy? Want to join me while I fix some lunch?"

Max lifted his head slowly and blinked before leaping up on all fours when he realized Sarah was speaking to him.

Woof! The enthusiastic wagging of his tail emphasized his acceptance of the invitation as he followed her downstairs to the kitchen.

"What sounds good today? Ham and cheese or leftover pizza?" she asked looking down at the golden retriever pressing his body next to her. His upturned nose twitched as she surveyed the contents of the refrigerator for potential meal options. She was reaching for the pizza when her phone rang.

"Sarah, it's Meghan. Would it be okay for me to crash at your house tonight?"

Sarah's parents, Kevin and Grace, were both professors and had accepted positions at the University of Maine, which meant they had to leave their home in Massachusetts, where

Sarah had lived all twelve years of her life. That was the year she and Meghan met. They were both the new kids in class that year and had instantly bonded. The friendship had lasted throughout their childhood and continued to the present day.

"Of course, but what's up? Aren't you still rooming with Lily?"

"I was."

She heard the hitch in Meghan's voice and became concerned.

"What's wrong, Meg?"

"It's Lily. She… she's dead!

Chapter 2

"*She's what?*" Sarah thought she must have misheard.

"She's dead. I... I came home and found her in our kitchen lying on the floor. She had a bash in her head. The police told me I can't stay here until the crime scene is investigated." Meghan managed to choke out between sobs.

"Oh, my gosh. Will you be able to drive, or should I come pick you up?"

"I'll drive myself. I don't want to be here any longer than I have to."

Something that Meghan said earlier niggled at Sarah and then it hit her. "Wait. Back up. Did you say *crime scene?*"

"I'll explain when I see you. Right now, I just want to leave as fast as I can."

⊏⊐

SARAH THOUGHT back to her college days when she and Meghan both attended the University of Maine but took different majors. That was where Meghan had met her roommate, Lily Sullivan. The three of them had often socialized and the idea of Lily being dead was surreal. And a *crime scene?* What the heck was going on?

Meghan arrived fifteen minutes later, overnight bag in hand. Her eyes were red-rimmed and puffy from crying.

"Come here," she said and wrapped her arms around Meghan when she saw the condition she was in. Sarah felt Meghan's body shake as she silently sobbed. They stood that way until at last, she regained control and only then did Sarah release her. "Why don't you take your bag upstairs to the guest room and I'll make us a cup of tea."

"Thanks. That sounds good."

Meghan put her suitcase on the bed and sat down beside it, her shoulders slumped, and her hands folded in her lap as she looked around at her surroundings. *I'm not sure how, but I guess things could be worse.* The soft pastels of the quilt on the queen size bed and the pale green walls felt peaceful. Two antique night-stands, lightly stained so the grain of the maple wood showed through, were adorned with small lamps and off-white crocheted doilies underneath them that looked old. She wondered if they'd belonged to either Sarah's or Ashley's grandmothers. The room was large enough that it had room for a comfy upholstered chair in one corner. She involuntarily let out a sigh as she considered her circumstances and then went downstairs.

The familiarity of the aroma of the Earl Grey tea had a calming effect on Meghan and restored a sense of normalcy to her when she returned to the kitchen where Sarah was pouring them each a mugful. She took a seat at the table covered with a cheerful yellow tablecloth and a small bouquet of orange and red mums which added to the coziness.

"Can you tell me what happened, or is it still too raw?" Sarah asked, placing Meghan's mug in front of her and then sitting down on the opposite side of the table facing her. Max curled up on the floor at her feet letting out a sigh, registering his disappointment that Sarah had still not made her lunch. If there were going to be any portions to share, he would have to wait.

"It might be best to tell you everything now."

Sarah nodded and waited quietly while Meghan took a long, slow breath to compose herself before she was ready.

"I had a craving for something sweet, so I checked the cookie jar to see if we had any, but I found a plastic bag filled with smaller bags of what were obviously drugs inside it instead of cookies. I guess I went a little off the deep end and started yelling at Lily, asking why she had them and what was she thinking? That it would be on both of us if the police raided the apartment because with that quantity of drugs, the only explanation would be that she was dealing. Lily began crying and telling me I didn't understand and that she could explain, but I didn't give her a chance. I was so angry I was afraid I would do or say something I would regret, so I told her to just save it and I was going to go out for a walk to cool off. I'm not even sure exactly where I went, but I ended up at the waterfront and it took me about an hour before I was ready to go back. By then I'd settled down and was calm enough for her to tell me the whole story because the Lily I know would never have been using drugs, much less selling them. I didn't think the *I'm holding them for a friend* line was the truth either, though, so what else could she say about why she had them? I was so confused." Meghan hesitated, searching Sarah's face for acknowledgement that she understood. Sarah remained silent, but nodded her head, encouraging Meghan to continue.

"When I got back, the door was unlocked, but I figured Lily must have left it open because I'd gone out without my keys. As soon as I stepped inside, I knew something was wrong. Usually, Panda would come running whenever Lily or I came into the apartment. I called out that I was back, thinking Lily might be in the bathroom, but she didn't answer. I got goosebumps on my arms because it was too quiet."

Sarah nodded once more when Meghan stopped talking, encouraging her to continue.

"I got this intuition that I should go into the kitchen and that's where I found her. I could tell she wasn't breathing, but I checked for her pulse anyway and she didn't have one. The cookie jar was open on the counter, but nothing was in it. She must have struggled with whoever was in the apartment with her because everything that had been on the table was strewn all over the floor."

Meghan burst into tears.

"Why didn't I give her a chance to explain? She might be alive if I'd been with her."

"Or they might have killed you, too," Sarah said. As soon as the words were out, it struck her that she was thinking in terms of a murder instead of an accident based solely on Meghan's description of the contents of the table being knocked off when she'd found Lily.

"They might have still been in the apartment. I didn't even think about that." Meghan's eyes widened and her sobs subsided as that settled in.

"What happened then?" Sarah asked.

"I went out in the hallway and called 911. I didn't want to be inside with..." Her lips flattened in a straight line as she fought to keep herself under control until she could continue. "The paramedics and the police came almost at the same time, maybe about five minutes later. Or it could have been sooner. It seemed like it took forever. They made me stay out of the apartment while they looked around, and then one of the cops asked for my statement. When we were finally done, I told them I needed to get back inside to look for Panda and had to explain that Panda is my cat. He said it would be okay as long as he was with me. We looked in every room, except for the kitchen, but couldn't find him and I was getting a little hysterical by then because the only thing I could think of was that he'd run outside when the killer left and he's not an outside cat. The cop told me I was going to have to let it go because we'd looked everywhere. Then he said I should pack a bag because I wouldn't be able to spend the night and I'd have to go someplace else to stay. He came into the bedroom and watched while I packed. I guess they wanted to make sure I wasn't taking any evidence with me. Then I called you and came right over."

Sarah thought about Meghan's account of the morning's events before speaking.

"What do you think now about whether Lily was dealing and if her murder was related?"

"I don't want to believe it, but considering what's happened, I don't know what else it could be."

Chapter 3

"Do you think we could go look for Panda?" Meghan asked later that afternoon.

Sarah didn't hesitate, knowing how she would feel if the situation was reversed and Max was missing.

"Of course. I'll leave Ashley a note in case she gets home before we do."

After half an hour of searching the yard and calling his name, they had no better luck than Meghan had had earlier.

She's not going to give up unless I put a stop to this. Sarah watched as Meghan retraced the steps they'd taken at least a dozen times already and her voice was hoarse from calling Panda's name over and over. Her eyes scanned the yard that was surrounded by a chain-link fence. *There's no way he's still here. He must have either jumped the fence or found another way out. That's not something I'm going to tell her, though.*

"I know you don't want to quit looking, but it's going to turn dark soon. We can come back first thing tomorrow morning." She thought she might have some pushback when she saw the look of determination on Meghan's face.

Instead, her shoulders slumped when the same look of determination was reflected back at herself from Sarah.

"Yeah, okay. If he hasn't come by now, he's probably not going to. He's never been outside by himself before, though. I hope he'll be alright…" her voice trailed off.

Me, too, or I'm going to feel like the biggest jerk in the world, Sarah thought as she walked to the car with Meghan trailing behind. "Why don't you make some posters when we get back and we can put them up tomorrow?" she asked, hoping it would reassure Meghan that she wasn't giving up on looking for Panda.

Meghan's face brightened. "That's a great idea! I've got loads of pictures of him on my phone. Would it be okay if I used your printer?"

"Absolutely!"

Neither spoke again for the remainder of the drive. By the time they got back, Ashley had returned, and they explained Meghan's presence. Although she hadn't known Lily as well as Sarah and Meghan, she had the same reaction of shock and disbelief upon hearing the news.

When Sarah announced that she would stay home that evening instead of attending her weekly quilt club meeting, they both insisted that she should go.

Several months earlier, Sarah had accepted an invitation to form a quilting club with three other women. They had all taken a class about free motion quilting at the local quilt shop, Quilting Essentials, and decided to continue their get-togethers every week even after the class ended. That decision had literally changed her life.

"We'll be fine, won't we, Meghan?" Ashley asked giving her a look that told her she had no other option even if Meghan had planned to say yes anyway.

"Sure. I'm probably going to just go to my room and read. It will help keep my mind off Lily and Panda."

Sarah took a long look at Meghan, skeptical she was being honest, but chose not to call her out on it. *Everyone has their own way of dealing with grief,* she reminded herself.

Saying her goodbyes, she picked up her sewing machine

and supplies along with a bag of quilts she'd placed in the coat closet earlier and drove to the meeting. They were contributions to a project the Cozy Quilts Club had organized to benefit the Linus Project. Each of the four members had volunteered to sew labels into them to identify the maker of the quilt. They'd been made to honor Summer Williams, a high school senior who had been struck and killed by a hit-and-run driver shortly before the school year began. The driver had been identified and arrested in large part through the efforts of the Club.

My life is so different since I met these women. A smile curved her lips as she thought of their first meeting. *I wish I could have seen my face. My chin must have been on the floor when Annalise outed us.* For most of their lives each of the women had hidden their unique abilities, but as a psychic, Annalise Jordan had tapped into them.

An image of herself at six years old popped into Sarah's head. It was recess at her elementary school when she approached the boy from her class who was about to climb the stairs to the slide. "Your grandmother wants me to tell you that you should give back the baseball card you stole from your brother."

Peter Wilson's eyes had nearly bugged out of his head. "You're lying. My grandmother is dead!"

"I know, but she's right here and she said you should know better. She told me to say she called you Peanut."

By this time a group of curious students had gathered around them, drawn to the drama playing out.

Peter's face was turning a bright shade of red, and his fists were clenched. *"Get away from me, you weirdo!* She says she's talking to my grandmother, but my grandmother is dead," his voice raised as he addressed the assembled crowd.

Ten faces turned to stare at Sarah, and then the chanting began. *Weirdo! Weirdo! Weirdo!*

Sarah winced at the memory. She'd tried a few more times

to pass along messages to others from deceased friends and relatives thinking Peter's reaction was unique. In her young mind, she'd reasoned he had reacted that way because she had told him where others could watch them, and he was embarrassed that he'd been caught stealing. After that, she made sure to pass along messages when it was only her and the person for whom the message was intended, but her efforts were rebuffed with the same response of horror and disbelief. She made a vow then that she would never tell anyone that she could talk to ghosts. It wasn't until her own grandmother's funeral, when Ashley knew something was wrong and pressed Sarah about it, that she reluctantly shared that secret. She'd felt that same confidence of trust with the Cozy Quilters as she had with Ashley, knowing she wouldn't be disbelieved or judged.

It's such a relief to be with people who understand what it's like to have to hide a part of yourself from most of the world. Sarah's shoulders and arms relaxed as the anxiety from that time in her life faded and was replaced with the sense of peace she now enjoyed.

Unbeknownst to most members of the communities of Glen Lake and Bangor, the four founding members had used their special skills to solve three murders. Not long after forming the club, they were drawn into their amateur sleuthing when member Jennifer Ryder's great aunt, Sadie Emerson, had been murdered.

Twenty minutes later, Sarah arrived at Eva Perkins's house where the meetings were held each week. Eva shared her home with her cat, Reuben. As an animal whisperer, she was able to communicate with him as well as with other animals. She often shared Reuben's snarky remarks with the group. Jennifer had the ability of psychometry, and the fourth member of the club was the psychic, Annalise Jordan.

"Is Sharon going to be coming?" Jennifer asked.

"She and Joseph went back to Arizona. They might be

back for the holidays but she probably won't make it to the meetings again until next spring," Annalise replied. Sharon was Annalise's cousin and had attended several of the Club's recent meetings.

"Paul called me earlier to say he won't make it tonight, either. He might not be able to come until after the holidays because it gets busy this time of year and he has to put in extra hours," Eva said. Paul was the machine technician from Quilting Essentials, the shop where they had attended the free-motion quilting class that brought them together.

"Alright, ladies, it's time to pick the theme for next month's project," Eva announced when they had finished with the Linus Project quilts. "Since it's October, should we choose something Halloween related?"

"I'd already been thinking about making a Halloween banner for our house and found a few patterns that were variations of a spider's web," Sarah said.

"Do you put it on a flagpole that's attached to your house?" Jennifer asked.

"Yes, exactly. We've been switching them out each month. They're mostly holiday-related so October and a Halloween theme was the first thing that came to mind."

"You know, I've been thinking of doing that same thing. I've got the perfect spot on my porch to put up a flagpole," Annalise joined in.

"It works for me, too. Should we make it official?" Eva asked.

Everyone joined in with a thumbs up.

"Do you have the pattern you picked to show us?"

"I think so, Jennifer." Sarah picked up her phone and scrolled to the spot where she saved the link and passed the phone to Jennifer. When Jennifer was done, she handed it over to Eva.

"That gives me some ideas to look up when I'm at home and I can use my laptop," Annalise said when she had finished inspecting Sarah's example. "Sarah, my intuition has been sending me signals all night long. Is something upsetting you?" she asked.

"Nothing gets by you, does it?" Sarah asked, teasing. "I hadn't planned to bring it up until I knew more. Earlier today I got a phone call from a friend of mine. She came back from a walk and discovered her roommate dead in their kitchen. The police wouldn't let her back into her apartment, so she asked if she could stay with me and Ashley. She asked if I could help. I don't have many of the details yet, but I think we may have another murder to solve," Sarah announced. "Meghan found drugs in their cookie jar... *I know, right?*" she said when she saw their raised eyebrows, "and Lily was the only person who could have put them there. They'd had an argument about it which is why she had gone out for the walk."

"Did you know Lily well?" Jennifer asked.

"Not as well as I know Meghan. We first met in grade school and have been best friends ever since."

"Do you think Lily could have been dealing?" Eva asked.

"I don't think so. It seems completely out of character from what I knew about her, but I don't know what else to think. She tried to tell Meghan she could explain, but she never got the chance."

A moment of silence passed as the ladies digested all they'd been told before Annalise spoke up to say, "I think we can help."

Chapter 4

Ashley had already left for work by the time Sarah and Meghan met in the kitchen the next morning. The aroma of coffee and toast lingered in the air. Rays of sunshine flooding through the window fell on the crystal vase in the center of the table, creating tiny rainbows. They were each lost in their own thoughts when the sound of Meghan's phone ringing made them both jump. Meghan frowned as she looked at the screen, not recognizing the number.

"Hello?" she answered, her voice hesitant and questioning.

"Meghan Doherty? This is Detective Lyndon Brooks. I've been assigned to the investigation of Lily Sullivan's death. Would you be available to come to the station for an interview?"

"Yes, of course. What time should I be there?"

They set the time for ten o'clock, and Meghan disconnected the call.

"That was the police. They want me to come down to the station for an interview."

"Would you like me to go with you? My schedule is flexible today."

"Would you?" Meghan asked and Sarah could see the worry on her face.

"Of course. They may not let me stay with you for the interview itself, but it might help you be less nervous knowing you've got a friend nearby."

Meghan rose from her chair and put her arms around Sarah, giving her a hug.

"It's going to be okay. We're going to figure this out." Sarah rubbed her hand on Meghan's back to reassure her. "I need to get a jump on my emails before we go," Sarah said, breaking the embrace. "I'm not expecting anything urgent but should probably check in case something came in overnight."

"Thanks, Sarah. I can't thank you enough for all you've done for me."

"That's what friends are for." Sarah gave Meghan what she hoped was a reassuring smile.

▭

TWO HOURS LATER, they arrived at the police station. Sitting at a desk in front of the back wall in the middle of the room was a woman in her forties with short, curly brown hair, dressed in civilian clothes. The wall behind her had a painting of the Maine state seal and photos of the governor and the current station commander on either side of it.

"If I didn't know better, I'd think we were in the waiting room of a car dealership," Sarah whispered, taking in their surroundings.

"Or a lawyer's office," Meghan whispered back.

To the left of the receptionist was a seating area that was equipped with a small coffee bar and a single serve hot water dispenser. It had an assortment of tea bags, coffees, and hot chocolate to choose from along with various sugars and powdered creamer, paper cups, and plastic lids. Missing were the stacks of magazines on a coffee table and plants that would be found in most office reception areas. The woman looked away from her computer monitor and turned to greet them.

"My name is Meghan Doherty. I have an appointment with Detective Brooks."

"And you are?" the woman, whose name plate identified her as Allison Cooper, asked Sarah.

"I'm Sarah Pascal, but I'm just here for moral support. He's not expecting me."

Ms. Cooper nodded her head and picked up the phone on her desk and punched in the extension for Detective Brooks. "A Meghan Doherty is here to see you."

After receiving his confirmation that she was expected, Ms. Cooper directed them to have a seat.

"It's going to be okay," Sarah quietly told Meghan. Her crossed legs were rapidly tapping the air to a silent beat that Sarah recognized as a tell when Meghan was nervous.

"I didn't even realize I was doing that," She smiled and stopped shaking her legs when she felt Sarah's hand on her knee.

They were soon greeted by Detective Brooks. Sarah guessed he was in his fifties. He was about six feet tall and easily forty pounds overweight, most of which was in his belly. His suit was rumpled and probably hadn't been to a dry cleaner for months.

Noticing how the buttons strained against his shirt placket creating small gaps, Sarah considered whispering to Meghan *How do those buttons manage to not pop off?* but thought better of it. If he heard, it might not go well for Meghan. *At least I can't see any bare skin behind them*, she thought and quickly looked away so he wouldn't notice her staring at his stomach.

"Ms. Doherty?" he asked, looking from one to the other.

"That's me. This is my friend, Sarah Pascal."

Brooks shook both their hands before addressing Sarah. "I'm going to have to ask you to wait here while we're doing the interview unless you're here as Ms. Doherty's legal representative."

"No, I'm just a friend. Will you be okay?" she asked Meghan, who nodded her affirmation. "I'll be right here," she said, giving her arm a squeeze.

After receiving a visitor badge from Ms. Cooper for Meghan and then swiping his badge to open the door situated to the right of the front desk, Detective Brooks led her down a hallway and into a conference room.

The room was sparsely decorated with only a rectangular wooden table and chairs with casters, one of which he pulled out for Meghan. In one corner of the room located at ceiling height was a camera. Once they had settled into their seats on opposite sides of the table, Brooks took a pen from his pocket and opened the file he had placed on the table when they'd walked in. Meghan caught a glimpse of one of the crime scene photos and quickly looked away.

"The report says you were the one who found Ms. Sullivan?" he began.

"Yes, that's right. I'd gone out for a walk and when I got back, I found her body in the kitchen," she said, taking a deep breath to compose herself and keep from crying.

"How long were you gone?"

"I didn't look at my watch when I left, but I'm guessing it was probably an hour."

"Where did you go?"

"I wasn't going anywhere in particular. I started walking and ended up down at the waterfront and then came back."

"Can anyone verify that?"

"I don't think so," she said, her anxiety ramping up. She'd watched enough television crime shows to suspect her alibi was being questioned.

"Your neighbors heard you arguing with Ms. Sullivan. What was that about?"

Meghan hesitated. She didn't want to get Lily in trouble,

but if she lied, it could come back on her. She swallowed but looked Brooks directly in the eye before answering.

"I found a bag of drugs in our cookie jar. I asked her why she had them and I got angry because it could have gotten both of us in trouble. Lily told me I didn't understand and tried to explain, but I cut her off and left the apartment to cool down. By the time I got home, it was too late. But the jar was empty, and the drugs were gone. The only thing I can think of was that someone came to take them back, and they must have had a fight because everything that had been on our table was strewn all over the floor."

"Was Ms. Sullivan a drug user?"

"No, never!"

"Are you sure? Why would she have drugs if she didn't use them. Was she dealing?"

"I don't know. Like I told you, I left before Lily could explain. I never saw her use drugs or be under the influence and I never saw her dealing drugs, so I have no idea why she had them."

"Do you use drugs, Ms. Doherty?"

"*What? No!*"

Brooks shuffled through the papers in his file. He already knew from the autopsy report the coroner had stated Lily's body had indications she had been pushed.

"According to one of your neighbors, your car was still in the parking lot, and no one noticed you leave the apartment building. Did things get out of hand when you argued? You got into a pushing match and Ms. Sullivan lost her balance and hit her head on the countertop? Maybe it was just an accident. You lost your temper and…"

Before he could finish, Meghan interrupted. "You think I killed Lily because we had an argument? I've never laid a hand on her. I don't care what we were fighting about. There is no way I would *ever* do something like that. Sure, I was angry, but that's why I left before things *did* get out of hand. I needed to cool off."

"Do you have a temper, Ms. Doherty?"

"Yes, but no worse than anyone else. I've never been physical with anyone I've argued with. I didn't leave because I was afraid I would hurt Lily physically. I left because I was afraid I would say something I couldn't take back." Meghan's stomach was tied in a knot and the color in her cheeks was rising. This was not going well.

Detective Brooks remained silent as he stared into Meghan's eyes. She could feel him challenging her to slip up and incriminate herself, but she held his gaze, knowing she was innocent, until at last, he looked down at his notes to confirm he hadn't missed anything. Satisfied, he looked up and asked, "That should be enough for now unless you have something else you'd like to add?"

"My cat, Panda, was inside when I went for my walk, but he wasn't there when I got back, and I haven't been able to find him since. He must have slipped out when whoever killed Lily left our apartment."

"Isn't it possible she let him out?"

"No. He's an indoor cat. Lily would never have done that."

"Cats can get by you if they're determined enough."

Meghan caught the dismissiveness in his voice. *There's no point trying to convince him there was someone else in the apartment who let Panda out. He's already made up his mind that didn't happen.* Her jaw tensed. She raised her chin defiantly and returned his stare but remained silent. *I'm not going to let him bully me. I'll wait for him to make the next move even if it takes all day.*

"I think this should wrap things up for today but please be sure to be available if we have any other questions."

Detective Brooks opened the security door to allow Meghan to pass through into the reception area, where Sarah was waiting. He didn't bother to say goodbye once she had walked through the door; he simply turned around to return to his office.

She was about to walk out when she heard Ms. Cooper asking, "Your visitor badge?"

"Oh, right. Here." Meghan handed the badge to Ms. Cooper, resisting the urge to toss it instead. *Don't take it out on her. It's not her fault he's a jerk.*

Sarah looked up from her laptop as Meghan approached but kept her expression blank when she saw her face.

"Let's get out of here," Meghan said, her voice quiet and brusque.

Sarah didn't speak until they reached her car.

"What happened in there?" she asked when they were both inside.

"I could be wrong, but I got the impression that Detective Brooks thinks I killed Lily when we argued. He suggested that I pushed Lily when we were fighting, and she hit her head on the countertop. None of the neighbors saw me leaving the apartment or when I got back, and my car was still in the driveway. In his mind, I made up the story about going out for a walk. Sarah, I'm scared. I don't think he'll even bother to look for anyone else. He's going to try to find anything that backs up his version of what happened so he can arrest me."

"What about the drugs?"

"He didn't seem interested in that either, especially when I said I'd never seen Lily using them or witnessed her dealing. My gut is telling me he thinks I made that up, too."

Sarah backed the car out of the parking space to drive back to her house. Meghan's head was turned away to look out the side window and, sensing that she needed time to process what had just happened, Sarah didn't press her further.

Chapter 5

"Would you two mind if I went out for a little bit? I need to go to Quilting Essentials to get fabric for my banner project. Or you're welcome to come with me," Sarah asked when they got back to her house.

"Thanks for the offer, but I think it's time for me to go back to the apartment. I got the okay from the police and Panda needs me. I know he's been missing a couple of days, but my intuition is telling me he's still nearby and hiding somewhere because he's scared. I'm going to sit out in the back yard and see if he'll come to me. Vivian is driving up today, so I should be there for her, too. The coroner has released Lily's body and Vivian is going to be making her funeral arrangements. I can't thank you both enough for all you've done for me."

Vivian Sullivan was Lily's older sister. They had been orphaned when Lily was a freshman in college and their parents were victims of a head-on collision by a drunk driver. Sarah had met her on several occasions when Meghan and Lily had parties to which she was invited.

"How is Vivian doing?" Sarah asked.

"Pretty much as expected. She's a wreck. This past year

she and Lily hadn't been as close. I don't know exactly what happened because Lily didn't want to talk about it whenever I would ask. They still spoke to each other on the phone and Lily drove down to Massachusetts at Christmas to be with Vivian, but it wasn't like when I first met them."

"Well, I wish you luck and don't be afraid to call us if there's anything we can do. And let us know when you have more information about the funeral," Ashley said, giving Meghan a hug, and Sarah did the same.

"Hi, Evelyn," Sarah greeted Evelyn Jackson, the owner of Quilting Essentials.

"Hi, Sarah. Is it time for a new project for the Cozy Quilts Club?"

"It is! I brought a copy of the pattern with me and was hoping you could help me pick out fabrics. I'm still not confident about that part of the process."

"Of course. How long have you been quilting?"

"My mom tried to teach my sister and me when I was about twelve. Hannah is two years older than me and has always been the crafty one, so she took right to it. My mom gave up on me when it was obvious I wasn't into it. All I wanted to do was spend time on our computer."

"That seems to have worked out for you. That's what you do for work, isn't it?"

"You've got a good memory. Yes, I'm a cybersecurity specialist and my company lets me work remotely with flexible hours. That comes in handy when I need to take time to do things like picking out fabric," Sarah said, smiling.

"Sounds like it works out for both of us," Evelyn returned her smile. "Did you have anything particular in mind for your project?"

Sarah retrieved the pattern from her purse to show Evelyn.

"It's more that I know what I *don't* want. The pattern is sewn as a scrappy project but it's not calling to me. At first I thought about going with white because it's a spider's web but that didn't appeal to me. Since it's for Halloween, my thought was to go with orange. What do you think?"

Evelyn took the pattern and looked through the directions.

"It would be easier to use a single color, but what would you think about using shades of orange to give it more interest? I happen to have a jelly roll in stock that would be perfect."

Sarah nodded as she considered Evelyn's suggestion.

"Yeah, I'd like to take a look at it so I can get more of a visual in my head."

Evelyn led the way to the section of the store where the pre-cut fabrics were displayed. Sarah's eyes scanned over the display of rolls of brightly colored strips of cloth, some solids and others beautifully color coordinated prints and batiks. Evelyn removed the one she had suggested for Sarah to inspect.

"The other nice thing about using a jelly roll is that it's already cut into the two-and-a-half inch wide strips so will save you some time," Evelyn suggested.

"That's true. And I see what you mean about how this would be more interesting with the variations, even though they're all orange," Sarah said as she turned the roll around to look at the different shades. "Sold!" she said once she'd finished.

"I think that will look great on a background of black. It will make the colors pop. And then with the black bias tape to outline the shape of the spider web, that will really make it stand out."

"Oh, right! I almost forgot; do you have that in stock?"

"We should. Let's go check."

Chapter 6

Meghan's hands shook as she tried to place her key in the lock. The door to the apartment next door opened and Brian Jackson stepped out, catching her by surprise. *Great. Just what I need now.* She forced herself to return his smile. He was a nice enough guy, but Meghan had been avoiding him as much as possible when she figured out he had a crush on her.

"Meghan, you're back! I've been worried about you."

"Thanks, Brian. I guess you know what happened with Lily. I had to leave until the police gave me the okay to come back."

"I did. I'm so sorry. Are you alright?"

She knew his concern was genuine, but she wasn't in the mood for chatting.

"That's so nice of you to ask. I'm doing okay. I need to go, but…" She was about to try once again to unlock her door, hoping that would clue him in that their conversation was over.

"I heard you and Lily fighting that day," he interrupted before she could finish her sentence.

Meghan's hand poised in mid-air. *Was he the neighbor who told Detective Brooks they'd overheard their argument?*

"Yes, we were," she said cautiously. "but I went out for a walk so we would both have time to settle down. I wasn't here when she died." Inspiration struck as another thought came to her. "Did you hear anyone else in our apartment?"

"No, I turned up the TV so I couldn't hear you. It made me upset."

"I'm sorry we upset you, Brian. The detective investigating the case seems to think I'm the one who killed Lily when we were fighting. Not intentionally, but that things got out of hand. I'm positive there had to be someone who came in after I went out for my walk, though. I was hoping you might have either seen or heard them." She wasn't about to tell him about a possible connection because of the drugs, but if he could corroborate her version about someone being in the apartment when she wasn't home, it might motivate Brooks to look for them.

His mouth opened as though he was about to say something but then he looked down and began to fidget.

What's that about? His fidgeting raised a red flag, but she couldn't put her finger on why.

"Oh, that reminds me! Have you seen Panda? He's been missing ever since I went out that day. I'm really worried because he's an inside cat."

"Oh, no! I haven't but I'll keep my eyes out."

"Thanks, Brian. You're a good neighbor. I should get my things put away. I want to go out to the backyard to see if I can find him," she said when he didn't make any moves to go back into his apartment.

"Do you need any help?"

Meghan's conscience twisted a little when she saw his hopeful expression.

"It's probably better if I do that alone. He has to be scared to death and if he spotted you there, he might not come to me."

"Oh, right, of course." His face fell and she felt another

twinge of guilt about hurting his feelings, but the last thing she wanted was his company. "Well, I'll leave you to it. I just wanted to make sure you were okay." He turned and walked back into his apartment without waiting for her to reply.

She knew the apartment had been cleaned by professional crime scene cleaners, but the thought of going back after what had happened caused her anxiety to ratchet up several notches. She took a deep breath to steady herself and on the next try, the key slipped into the lock, and she slowly pushed the door open. The astringent odor of disinfectant was the first thing she noticed, and a wave of nausea mixed with sadness came over her, thinking of the reason for the odor. She hurried straight to her bedroom to put her overnight bag away, averting her eyes from the kitchen as she passed by.

You're going to have to face this sooner or later, she chided herself. In the meantime, her first priority was finding Panda. She walked down the stairs and out to the common area in the back of the apartment building and sat in one of the Adirondack chairs shared by all the tenants. She called Panda's name and pursed her lips making the universal mwah sound made by humans to call their pets, and then waited, listening intently for any noises indicating he was nearby. She tried again with the same results. Discouraged, she leaned back in the chair and looked up at the overcast sky. *Great, rain's coming. What else can go wrong?* Her heart sank. One more thing to add to the long list of bad news of the last couple of days. It didn't look like it was going to rain soon, but the clouds bore the promise of a storm brewing. *Maybe it will hold off until Panda returns*, her optimistic side chimed in. Her gut was still telling her he was here, probably hiding in the shrubbery that ran around the perimeter of the fenced yard. Her thoughts were drifting to the argument between her and Lily, wishing for the thousandth time she hadn't walked out, when she was brought back by what she thought was a faint mew. Not sure if it was only her imagination, she called Panda's name again.

"Come on out, Panda. It's okay. I'm right here."

Her eyes scanned the lot looking for any sign that he was there but found nothing. She was about to give up when her ears tuned into a rustling of leaves from the far-left corner of the fencing and then one paw and Panda's head appeared as he crawled out from under the bush.

Meghan's eyes filled with tears and her first reaction was to run to him, but just as she was about to leap out of the chair she stopped. *That might scare him*, her instinct kicked in. Instead, she leaned over and quietly snapped her fingers and made the mwah noises again to call him to her. Their eyes locked and that was all it took for Panda to break into a run, and she scooped him up in her arms, nuzzling her face into his fur.

"Oh, Panda. I'm so happy to see you. Let's take you inside. You must be so scared and you're probably starving."

Panda butted his head into her face and began to purr, his body vibrating with their intensity as she took him back to the apartment and quickly shut the door behind them to prevent him from escaping again. His body stiffened as soon as they entered the apartment and Meghan knew that he must have witnessed what happened to Lily.

"It's okay, buddy. It's just us. You're safe."

Her stomach tightened as she walked into the kitchen, and it occurred to her that that reassurance applied to her as well. She held him in one arm as she poured kibble in his bowl with the other and then set him down to fill his water dish. Panda looked as though he was about to bolt, but hunger overruled and slowly at first, he nibbled at the food.

"Slow down, buddy. You're going to make yourself sick," Meghan admonished as he began to gobble the kibble and picked up the bowl, placing it on the countertop to give him a chance to digest what he'd already eaten. She was rebuked with a loud meow imploring her to put it back down, but she resisted. "I'll give you more, but not yet."

Meghan picked him up and scratched under his chin and

around his ears, soliciting another round of purring. She walked with him into the living room and sat down on the comfy couch and he curled up on her lap, his paws tucked beneath his chin. She stroked his back, the motion relaxing her shoulders and she almost felt at ease when there was a knock on the door.

Chapter 7

"*Oww!*" she burst out when Panda's claws poked through her jeans and dug into her skin. He jumped up and sped into the hallway leading to the safety of the bedrooms, and she knew he would be hiding under either Lily's bed or hers.

With butterflies in her stomach, she walked as quietly as possible toward the door, hoping whoever was on the other side wouldn't hear her. Rising up on her tiptoes, she peeked through the peephole and was relieved to see Vivian.

"Vivian, I'm so sorry," Meghan said as she hugged Vivian tightly even before she could enter the apartment. Vivian hugged her back just as tightly before extricating herself to reach down for her overnight bag as Meghan stood aside to let her in.

"I guess I should put this in Lily's room."

"I'll put on some coffee. Unless you want something else?"

"Coffee's good," Vivian answered. "I'm pretty tired from the drive so that might help."

A few minutes later Vivian reappeared in the kitchen and sat at the table.

"That smells heavenly," she said as Meghan poured them each a mug.

Vivian kept her eyes down as she stirred her coffee. There was an awkward silence as they sat, each waiting for the other to begin until Vivian looked up into Meghan's eyes.

"I've heard the police's side of the story, but what really happened?"

"I'm so sorry, Vivian. I should have stayed and let Lily explain. I was being completely selfish and thinking about the trouble I would be in if she was caught with the drugs in our apartment," Meghan said after she had told Vivian about that part of their argument. "I probably should have mentioned this when I called to tell you about Lily. I think a part of me was protecting her. I thought if you knew about the drugs, it would upset you."

Vivian nodded, considering her words before she replied. "When our parents died, we both were devastated, but we dealt with it differently. I'm four years older so I took it upon myself to step into their shoes. That wasn't what Lily needed at nineteen years old, but I was too young myself to figure that out at first. She'd always been a good kid and didn't get into any trouble, so when I tried telling her what to do, she rebelled. It was a natural reaction and the more she acted out, the more I tried to rein her in. That's where we were at when you met her at the sorority. She was a bit of a wild child." They both smiled thinking back on those days. "It took me a while but, with some counseling, I realized the harm it was doing for both of us in our relationship and I backed off. We talked about it and I apologized. That cleared the air and Lily turned herself around. By the time you two graduated, we were back to how it had been before, and I couldn't have been prouder of her. When you two first got this apartment, I bit my tongue so I wouldn't butt in about telling you how I thought you should do things. The first time I came back to visit, and you had set everything up, I couldn't believe what a great job you'd both done. You were being smart about your budget and had gone to consignment shops for a lot of your furniture instead of having to buy everything brand new. And look around at this place, you've made it your *home*, not just an apartment. Everything was going great. Until it wasn't. You've probably noticed that Lily and I hadn't been keeping in touch as much as we used to."

Meghan nodded. "I mentioned it in passing to Lily, but she didn't want to talk about it, and I could see there wasn't any point in trying to push her, so I let it slide. I figured it was one of those sibling things and you'd both get over it."

"We had a fight about drugs, too. I'd become suspicious about some of her behavior and there were a few times when something she said made me think drugs were involved. She got really defensive when I asked her about it and told me I was imagining it. Things weren't the same between us after that, though. When I came up this summer, she suggested we go out for a drink and insisted we go to a bar called Riverside down on Main Street. When we got there, I didn't want to go in because it was so sketchy on the outside. She said if I didn't want to go in, she'd go by herself, so I went with her despite my better judgement. When we got inside it was even worse, but she headed straight for a booth in the back like she'd been there before. She made sure to sit so that she was facing the door and kept looking that way like she was waiting for someone. We'd been there about ten minutes when she grabbed her purse and told me to wait in the booth while she used the bathroom. I turned around when she left and saw her heading toward a guy who must have just walked in, and he followed her toward the bathrooms. She came back to the booth a few minutes later and didn't even bother to sit down, just told me we should leave. She didn't have to ask me twice, but I knew something was wrong. Once we got outside and were walking back to our car, I asked her what was going on but all she would say was that she couldn't talk about it, and I should drop it. I asked her pointblank if she was into drugs. She got really upset and told me again to drop it, so I did. Before I left to go home, she asked me if I still had the key to the safe deposit box that is in both our names, which I do. And then she told me if anything ever happened to her, there would be an envelope in it for me."

The implications of what that could mean settled over Meghan.

"What was Lily into, Vivian?"

"I don't know but I'm going to find out."

Chapter 8

"It's too late to go to the bank and, honestly, I'm too exhausted both physically and emotionally to deal with this today. Would you be able to go with me tomorrow?" Vivian asked.

They had moved to the living room where it was more comfortable. Meghan had pulled her legs up onto the couch and was slightly turned to face Vivian who was sitting at the other end. She was feeling more at ease now that she knew Vivian had also suspected Lily's involvement with drugs.

"Sure, I'd be happy to. I still have another day of bereavement leave. Normally, I wouldn't qualify, but because of the circumstances, my employer approved it."

"Thanks, Meg. Lily always thought the world of you. Despite what happened between you that day, I don't think that would have changed."

Meghan's eyes teared up and it took all she had in her not to cry. After how they'd left things, she wasn't sure she deserved to be told those words. Seeing her distress, Vivian reached out her hand and Meghan took it in hers. Neither of them spoke, nor needed to.

It was the sound of a loud meow that broke the mood and made them both laugh.

"There you are! It took you long enough to come out. Are you hungry again?" Meghan asked, reaching down to stroke Panda's back when he jumped up beside her.

Meow!

"I take it that's a yes."

"He's such a handsome guy. I've always meant to ask why you named him Panda."

"It's because he's black and white. I thought about calling him Tuxedo, but it didn't suit him. It was too formal but when I thought about calling him Panda, it felt right."

The cat padded into the kitchen following close behind Meghan and purred appreciatively when she set his food dish back on the floor.

"I'm going to trust you not to eat too fast."

Meghan explained to Vivian that Panda had been missing since the day Lily was killed and she had only found him earlier that day.

"He must have been frightened to death! He probably saw what happened," Vivian realized.

"That's what I think, too. If only you could talk, Panda."

Chapter 9

Vivian and Meghan arrived at the bank shortly after it opened the next day. It was a small branch office on the other side of town from the apartment. On the right were two offices with glass walls facing the interior and vertical blinds that could be closed for privacy. In the middle was a counter with slots for deposit and withdrawal slips and a wire mesh cup filled with pens bearing the bank's name and logo. Three teller stations were located on the opposite wall but only two tellers were on duty, one of whom shifted between his station and the drive-up window. Vivian explained her reason for being there to the other teller and was directed to the manager who also functioned as the customer service agent.

"I'll wait here in the lobby. I don't think I can go in with you since I'm not on the account," Meghan said.

"You're probably right. I don't think this will take long, though."

After providing her identification and signing in, Vivian was led into the vault where the safe deposit boxes were located. She handed her key to the manager who unlocked the door with the corresponding bank key and slid the box out of its compartment.

"Would you like to take the box to the conference room?"

"I think I'll be fine here," Vivian told her but waited until the manager left before opening the lid.

The only item inside was a thick manilla envelope with Vivian's name written on the outside. She slid the contents that included a journal, a key, and several USB drives, onto the counter. *This will have to wait until we're back at the apartment. It will take too long to figure out here.* She put everything back into the envelope and dropped it into her purse.

Vivian closed the lid of the box and slid it into the empty compartment so the manager would not realize it was empty, even though it was entirely within her rights to remove the contents.

"Is there anything else I can help you with today?" the manager asked.

"I think that should do it," Vivian said giving the manager a smile and met Meghan in the lobby.

"Let's go home," was all she said.

During the drive, Vivian was deep in her own thoughts and respecting her space, Meghan held her questions. Once back inside, Vivian took the envelope out of her purse.

"Let's take it into the kitchen so we can spread things out on the table."

"Sure thing. I'll make us some room," Meghan said, and removed the napkin holder and small floral arrangement.

Vivian spread the contents on the table and decided to open the journal first. She found a piece of paper folded in thirds tucked inside the front cover. She unfolded it and discovered it was a letter written in Lily's handwriting which she read aloud for Meghan's benefit.

Vivian,

At the risk of being melodramatic, if you're reading this, it means that I'm dead. I'm sure you must have a lot of questions and I hope this journal will answer them for you. It probably also means that I'm being framed for being a drug dealer and although that is technically true, there's more to the story.

I never meant to get involved with drugs. I was having some trouble paying my student loans and the interest charges were starting to pile up. I was too embarrassed to ask you for help because I thought you would be upset that I'd maxed out all my credit cards and couldn't keep up with the payments on those plus my student loans. Someone I thought was a friend told me about a guy he knew who could give me a short-term loan. It all sounded great, and I thought I'd be able to catch up again and it would be a one-time thing. I didn't realize the guy was a loan shark and the only way I could get out from under the loan was to agree to deal drugs for him. At first, I didn't know what else to do so I went along with it. He had an enforcer who threatened to hurt both you and Meghan if I didn't.

A couple months ago, I got caught by a DEA agent. He told me if I became an informant, they wouldn't file any charges and it wouldn't even appear on my record. They're aware the drug ring is being run by a crooked cop, but they don't have his name and they wanted to use me to find out who it was.

The USB drives have copies of recordings I made during the deals, and I've written down dates and names along with the drugs they had me selling. I'd hoped I'd never have to use it, but if you're reading this, things went south. The agent's name and how I contact him is in the journal, too. Get in touch with him and tell him I'm sorry, but maybe this information will help. There are two recordings he hasn't heard with someone I'd never seen before. I didn't find out who the cop was, but we were so close.

I'm sorry we've drifted apart the past few months. If I could have told you what was going on, I would have but I'd been warned not to say anything. I hope you believe how much I love you and that you will forgive me when you've learned the truth.

Lily

P.S. One more thing, don't trust anyone at the police. If the dirty cop finds out, he might hurt you, too.

Chapter 10

"Why don't you read through the journal? I'll get my laptop and headphones so I can listen to the recordings," Meghan said. They compared notes when they'd finished but neither of them had found anything in either the journal or the recordings that provided them with any conclusive proof about who might have been the ones who'd been in the apartment the day Lily died.

"I suppose that's to be expected," Meghan said. 'We have no context for all this information. Do you think we should get in touch with the DEA agent?"

Vivian considered that option. "I think we should. He may already have been told about this but if he hasn't, it's important that he finds out how Lily was killed. The cops might have found out she was working for the DEA, and he could be in danger now, too."

"I hadn't thought of that, but you're right."

They found the entry with his contact information and Vivian dialed the number. It rang four times before going to voice mail, but she hung up rather than leaving a message when the greeting advised that he was currently on vacation.

"Now what?" Vivian asked.

"I've got an idea. Let's get this packed up and I'll explain on the way."

Vivian's eyebrows scrunched up in confusion, but she followed Meghan's lead and helped pack the journal and USB drives into a paper bag and followed her out of the apartment.

Meghan was deep in thought as they walked to the parking lot and Meghan's car, but Vivian couldn't wait any longer.

"Okay. Earth to Meghan. What's the plan and where are we going?"

"What? Oh, sorry," Meghan said coming out of her reverie. "I think we should give this to Sarah."

"Why Sarah?"

"She works for a cyber-security company so she has the skills to make copies of the journal and recordings and store them so nobody could hack into them. This might be why they killed Lily. They could have found out she was working for the DEA and was recording their conversations. We can't risk something happening to them if there's no backup files, or everything Lily did would be for nothing," Meghan explained.

"That's a good idea. Is that where we're going now?"

"Right. The sooner we give it to her, the sooner it will be safe."

They arrived at Sarah's house thirty minutes later and knocked on the main door located inside the covered porch. Vivian turned to Meghan with fear in her eyes, when the commotion of a dog barking loudly and someone telling it to shush came through from the other side of the door.

"It's okay. Max is a sweetheart," Meghan reassured her.

As soon as the words were out of her mouth, Max had the opportunity to prove that when the door opened and he squeezed past Sarah, tail wagging and a big grin on his face.

"Hello, Max," Vivian said, as she put out her hand for him to sniff and the golden retriever obliged, giving it a lick.

"Come on, Max, let them in, it's cold out here! I'm sorry about that," Sarah apologized but Vivian waved it away.

"He's fine." She said, patting his soft fur.

"I'm so glad you found Panda!" Sarah told Meghan, who had texted her earlier to give her the news he'd returned.

"I have no idea if he was there the whole time when we were looking for him, but the little stinker was hiding under a bush at the far end of the yard. I think it must have been hunger that finally got him to come out. He was scared when we first came in, but he seems pretty happy to be back in the apartment now. I think he may have seen what happened. I told Vivian it's too bad he can't talk."

Sarah only smiled but the comment gave her the idea to speak with Eva. It would mean revealing her ability to communicate with animals to another outsider and she wanted her permission first. Panda might not be able to tell them anything that would identify who killed Lily, but it was worth a try. It had worked once before when the dog's owner had told Eva the name of her killer.

She embraced Vivian and whispered, "I'm so sorry for your loss. Lily was a smart, beautiful woman and she didn't deserve this."

"Thank you," Vivian replied, her voice barely a whisper as a wave of emotion overcame her.

"Let's go in the living room where it's more comfortable and you can tell me about what you wanted me to see."

Vivian handed the envelope to Sarah, explaining how she came to have it in her possession.

"This is evidence that could prove Lily was working with the DEA. We tried contacting the agent she was working with but got a voice mail message saying he is on vacation. Meghan had the idea that you could store this on the cloud in a secure location in case anything ever happened to the original."

Sarah looked from Meghan to Vivian, not sure how to process what she'd been told.

"Of course, but why don't you take it to Detective Brooks?"

"Lily warned me not to go to the police because the drug ring is run by a dirty cop. She didn't know who it is, so neither do we. We can't take any chances that the evidence would be destroyed. She said one of the recordings has new information the DEA agent hasn't heard."

"Wow! You're absolutely right, this needs to be protected. I'll set up a file with extra security. Do you think Brooks might be involved? He didn't seem to be in any rush to find another suspect for Lily's killer. He might be trying to frame you."

"Lily didn't mention him, so I can't be sure. If he is involved, though, being framed is what I'm afraid of, too."

Chapter 11

Sarah called a special meeting of the Cozy Quilts Club to ask
for their help now that she had learned more about a possible
motive for Lily's murder.

"Meghan gave me an idea although she didn't realize it,"
Sarah began, telling them about her offhand comment about
Panda. "Would you be willing to meet with Panda to see if
there's anything he could tell you? You had such good luck
with Boscoe, I thought it might work again. It would mean
telling Meghan and possibly Vivian that you can talk to
animals, and I would understand if that's not something
you're willing to do."

"I'm okay with that. Talking to Boscoe helped solve Sadie
Emerson's murder. If it means finding out who Lily's killer
was, risking the embarrassment of having someone outside of
our group know I talk to animals would be worth it."

"And now we have Phil and Dennis on our side so we
wouldn't have to prove we're not making it all up if we called
them to help," Jennifer said.

Detectives Phil Roberts and Dennis Smith had been
assigned to the three murder cases that the Cozy Quilts Club
had played an instrumental part in solving. They had been

skeptical at first but had been the ones to approach the Club members to ask for help when they had run out of clues to find Summer Williams's killer. The Club members knew it had taken a lot for the detectives to ask as it meant admitting they finally believed their paranormal abilities must be real.

"They're not assigned to this case, but at least we don't have any reason to think we can't trust them. Lily warned Vivian that a dirty cop is part of the drug ring and her killer could be part of the police department," Sarah informed them.

"Have you considered contacting Lily directly, Sarah?" Annalise asked.

A look of stunned realization crossed Sarah's face and she did a face palm.

"That's so obvious now that you say it," she replied. "What do you all think? Should we have Eva try first or maybe we could both go at the same time? I'm not sure how Meghan or Vivian would react this soon after Lily's death. We could hold it as a plan B."

"Is Meghan aware you have the ability to communicate with the dead?" Eva asked.

"No. It's not that I'm trying to hide it from her but I never had a reason to bring it up before. I don't have any problem telling them if it would help, and Meghan and Vivian are okay with it. It might be a lot for them to process."

"I think we should at least give them the option," Annalise said.

"Agreed," Eva put in.

"Okay, then, I'll give Meghan a call right now to…"

Before Sarah could finish her sentence, her phone began to ring. "Speak of the devil," she said for the others' benefit.

"Meghan, I was just about to call you."

"They're gone! The journal and the USB drives are gone!"

Chapter 12

"What do you mean, they're gone?"

"Vivian and I decided to go out for a pizza, and she put the envelope on Lily's bed. She was going to go to the bank tomorrow to put it back in the safe deposit box, but when we got home, it was missing. Someone had to have come in and taken it but there's no sign that they broke into the apartment. It's like that was the only thing they were after."

"Have you called the police?"

"No. After what Lily put in her letter, we don't trust them. And I forgot to mention the door was locked. Brooks already thinks I'm making it up about Lily and the drugs."

"Did you mention the journal and drives or the key to anyone else?"

"No, you're the only one."

The implications of that ran through Sarah's mind. She was even more relieved that they had decided she should keep the key since they couldn't make a copy of it digitally.

"Okay. I have an idea, but I don't want you to say anything more. I want you and Vivian to meet me at my house in half an hour. Don't say my name or where you're

46

going. Just hang up now and I'll explain everything when I see you," she immediately cautioned.

Three expectant faces were all staring at Sarah.

"Meghan's apartment was broken into. The envelope with Lily's journal and the USB drives is gone. Nothing else is missing so that had to be what they were after. I think her apartment might be bugged and it's possible they have a key since the door was locked when they got home."

The tension in the room heightened as the expression on each of their faces reflected their understanding. Annalise felt her body tingle and the hair on her arms began to rise as she considered the danger Meghan and Vivian were facing. She would have to give this more thought when she returned home and could have a quiet spot to meditate.

"If that's the case, it might not be wise to contact Panda or Lily in their apartment. Or at least not yet," Eva warned. "I don't suppose you know how to check for bugs?" she asked Sarah, although she already assumed the answer would be yes.

"More to the point is that I don't have that kind of equipment. But, fortunately, I have a friend who does."

"This is getting serious. I think we should get in touch with Dennis and Phil to ask for their help," Jennifer said.

"They might not be able to become involved since it's not their case but at the very least it's worth asking them," Annalise agreed.

"Would you do that, Jennifer? You've had the most contact with them," Sarah asked.

"I'll call first thing in the morning unless you think I should do that tonight."

"Tomorrow's fine. I'll need to call my contact about the bug sweep tomorrow, too. I should get going now. I want to be at my house when Meghan and Vivian get there. I should text Ashley to tell her they're coming in case they get there before I do, though."

Plans in place, Jennifer, and Annalise said their goodbyes as well.

"Be careful," Annalise cautioned. "You don't know what, if anything, these criminals have found out about how much you're involved."

"I will," Sarah replied and decided not to ask if Annalise was foreshadowing something sinister. It might be nothing, but for now she didn't want to know.

Chapter 13

"I have to go back to work tomorrow. Will you be okay by yourself in the apartment?" Meghan asked Vivian. Her tone was calm, but her expression showed her concern.

They were sitting in Sarah and Ashley's living room with Max stretched out on the couch between them, softly snoring. The room carried the faint smell of citrus emanating from the candle wax warmer on the end table. Had it not been for the undertone of tension in the room, it would have made a cozy tableau.

"I should be okay. It seems like they got what they wanted." The quaver in Vivian's voice betrayed the confidence she was trying to convey.

"Why did you want us to come here, Sarah? Couldn't we have just talked on the phone?"

"I suspect your apartment might be bugged. It's the only reason I can think of that whoever took the envelope would have found out you had it, *and* known it was something that could implicate them in the drug deals."

Meghan reached out to grasp Vivian's hand for comfort and support.

"How would we find out?" Vivian asked.

"I can get in touch with someone who has the equipment to sweep for bugs if you're okay with that."

"Of course! When could they come?" The fear in Meghan's voice was obvious.

"Hank told me he could come tomorrow. The only repercussion I can think of is that removing it might tip them off that you've figured out they're there. It might be better to wait until Lily's killer is captured, but without any suspects, that could take a while. You should call a locksmith to have your lock changed, too. There's a good chance they have a key to the apartment if they were able to let themselves inside without breaking in and lock the door back up when they left."

"I'll take care of changing the lock first thing tomorrow while you're at work," Vivian offered.

Meghan had released Vivian's hand and now rubbed her own hand mindlessly over her arm, weighing her options before answering. "I think we should get rid of the bugs now," she said, looking toward Vivian for her agreement, and she nodded her head. "I don't think I would be able to stay in the apartment otherwise knowing there was someone listening to everything that was being said. They've got the envelope and her journal and recordings. They must have heard you read Lily's letter, so they know she warned us about going to the police. I'm so glad we brought them to you to make copies. At least we've got those and the key, if we can ever find out what it goes to."

"I may have a way to find out," Sarah said.

Chapter 14

"What I'm about to tell you is going to be difficult to believe, but please hear me out. My quilt club friends, and I have more than quilting in common. We each have skills that most others don't. We've used them to solve three murders since we first began our monthly get-togethers."

Sarah then went on to tell Megan and Vivian exactly how the four women had solved the cases using their paranormal talents. When she finished, the room was so quiet they could have heard the proverbial pin drop. Even Max's snoring had stopped.

Meghan's expression went from disbelief to exasperation, and finally to anger.

"Come on, Sarah. This isn't something to joke about. Vivian and I could be in real danger. You don't seriously expect us to believe you."

Sarah remained calm, recognizing she had taken a risk telling them about the secrets she and the others had been keeping most of their lives. Meghan's reaction wasn't far off from what she'd expected.

"I meant it when I said it would be hard to believe, but I'm not joking. Maybe you would be more willing to believe me if you meet Dennis Smith and Phil Roberts. They were the homicide detectives involved with all three cases and were skeptical, to say the least, but they've accepted that we're legit. When you called, I was with the Club, and we were discussing the benefits of asking them to help us with Lily's murder even though they aren't assigned to it. They'd probably have to be careful about how much involvement they have, but it might be our only choice given how Detective Brooks hasn't exactly broken any speed records trying to find another suspect."

"That's an understatement!" Meghan scoffed. "Are you sure they can be trusted?"

"I'm sure."

"It's okay with me if it's okay with Vivian."

"As far as approaching the detectives, I agree it would be worth talking to them. It might not lead anywhere, but at least we'd have the satisfaction we've tried while we're waiting for the DEA agent to be back on duty. I honestly don't have any idea of what to say about the other... stuff... you told us," Vivian said.

Sarah nodded with understanding, and then a light switched on in her brain.

"I've got an even better person for you to talk to who was a skeptic but has become a believer. Eva's partner, Jim Davis, is a retired state police officer. He had a first-hand experience with Eva and her cat, Reuben. When we were working on our first case, she needed to convince him about her ability to communicate with animals, so she did a demonstration for Jim. Jennifer, Annalise, and I have all learned information through our abilities that we couldn't have gotten otherwise, and it's been instrumental in solving other cases. Would it be enough to convince you if all three cops tell you they believe us?"

"What do you think, Meg? Should we trust them?"

Meghan still looked dubious but shrugged her shoulders.

"I guess it couldn't hurt to at least listen. What have we got to lose?"

Chapter 15

"Jim is on board. I'll pick you up at ten and take you to Eva's house. She came up with the idea of doing the same kind of demonstration for you as she did with Jim. If you can see it with your own eyes, it might be more believable than his just telling you about it."

"Sounds good. I'll meet you downstairs."

"That was Sarah. She's going to pick me up at ten. I promise I'll give you a full report tonight when you get home from work," Vivian told Meghan.

"Do you think Sarah is telling the truth about all of this? It seems so far-fetched. In all the years I've known her, she's never mentioned she could talk to dead people."

"I thought about that a lot last night after we left her house. What I finally decided was that she has no reason to lie about it and she doesn't seem like the kind of person who would pull a prank on a friend, especially for something as serious as this. There's a part of me that really wants to believe she can talk to Lily so she can tell her for me how much I love her and miss her and how sorry I am about how I treated her when I found out about the drugs. I should have known better than to judge her like that."

⊏▭⊐

"COME IN, COME IN," Eva said when they arrived at her house, gesturing for them to come in. "You must be Vivian. I'm so sorry for your loss," Eva said and embraced Vivian, who was momentarily taken aback at the display of affection. "I hope this won't be too much for you. I realize it's a lot to take in. Jim is in the living room. Can I get either of you something to drink?"

"Take a breath, Eva," Sarah chuckled after being bombarded with Eva's non-stop greeting. "I don't need anything to drink. I had breakfast right before coming here."

"Nothing for me, either, but thank you for the offer."

"Well, then, follow me." Eva led them over to where Jim was waiting, and Vivian relaxed as soon as she entered without even being consciously aware it happened when the room's calming vibe took hold.

Jim stood up from the couch to introduce himself when he noticed them coming. "I'm Jim Davis. I'm so sorry for your loss of your sister."

"Thank you," Vivian replied. "It still hasn't sunk in completely that she's gone."

"Oh, the cookies!" The aroma of fresh baked cookies was in the air and Eva excused herself to bring them some. No one needed a second invitation to take one when she passed around the plate, despite Sarah and Vivian's earlier statement that they had just had breakfast. Once Eva sat to join the others, Jim was the first to speak, breaking the awkward silence that hung in the room.

"Sarah told me you've come so I can tell you about my experience with Eva's ability to speak to animals. I like to tell myself that I have an open mind but when she told me she could talk to Reuben—and other animals—I was skeptical and thought she was pulling my leg at first. I felt pretty foolish but agreed to the demonstration to humor her. After she repeated to me what I had told Reuben while she was at the other end of the house, I became a believer. I hadn't told anyone what I told him, but Reuben repeated exactly what I'd said."

Vivian still looked doubtful, but she didn't get the sense from Jim that he was lying. Still, it was possible that Eva could have overheard him. "Are you sure she couldn't hear you?"

"Absolutely! I was sitting right where I am now, and I spoke just above a whisper. Her hearing is fine, but she doesn't hear *that* well to be able to catch what I said from the back of the house."

"Would you like to see where I was while they were talking?" Eva offered.

"Erm, okay," Vivian looked at Sarah but said nothing before following Eva through the dining room and kitchen and finally entering the screen room. "I see what Jim was saying. You'd have to have exceptional hearing to know what he said from this far away," she admitted.

"How about this? Is there something you and Sarah might each know that she could tell Reuben while you wait in here. And Jim and I will wait here with you, too, so there's no chance that we could listen to what she's saying either."

Vivian considered the suggestion and then slowly nodded her head. "Should Sarah and I talk about it first or would it be better if she picked something so even I won't know what it was?"

"I think Sarah picking something without you two talking about it first sounds like a great idea! We should go back to the living room together so you can be certain that Sarah hasn't told me what it is while you're in here. Then we can tell Jim and Sarah what we're going to do."

As Eva explained the plan to her and Jim, Sarah glanced over at Vivian. Her expression said everything that needed to be said to confirm she was still skeptical. A smile slowly spread across Sarah's face. "I figured out exactly what I'm going to tell Reuben."

"Oh! I've got another idea! You two wait here and I'll be right back. Reuben," she said addressing the gray Maine coon cat sitting on a cushion in the bay window, "you know the drill. Do what you did with Jim."

Do I have any choice? I'm beginning to resent being put on display to perform tricks like a circus animal. His tone didn't leave any doubt about his displeasure, but he jumped down and padded over to sit in front of Sarah, looking up at her with his green eyes narrowed. *Alright. Let's get this over with.*

"Now, Reuben, you know I don't think you're a circus animal and I wouldn't ask you to do this if it wasn't important."

Reuben had turned his head in Eva's direction while she spoke. When she'd finished, he blinked his eyes and then turned back to Sarah as though to dismiss Eva. Vivian watched their interaction with curiosity, but it wasn't enough to make her reconsider her opinion.

"I'll only be a minute."

Eva returned holding a white noise machine in her hands. "It occurred to me that we could put this on for good measure while Sarah is talking to Reuben to block out any sound coming from here. Are you ready?" she addressed Sarah and Reuben after plugging it in. Sarah nodded but Reuben ignored Eva and continued to stare at Sarah instead.

"Okay, let's get this show on the road," she said to Jim and Vivian. "Sorry, Reuben. That just slipped out," she said noticing him glaring at her.

Once they left, Sarah turned on the white noise machine and looked at Reuben. "Even though I know this isn't fake, it's still a little weird."

That coming from the woman who talks to dead people, Reuben thought, but realized the irony was lost on Sarah without Eva to translate for him.

"Okay, when Meghan, Lily, and I were in college, we went on a girls' trip during the March Madness break week and Vivian was invited, too. We found a package deal for the airfare and hotel that we couldn't pass up to go to Las Vegas and there was a lot of drinking involved. We got tossed out of one of the casinos and Lily almost got arrested. Since then, we've taken the 'what happens in Vegas, stays in Vegas' motto to heart, and made a pact never to say anything to anyone else. I hope Vivian will think this situation warrants an exception." She looked at Reuben not sure how to proceed. Should she ask him if he got all that and wait for a sign? He blinked at her almost as though he had read her mind and was telling her to call the others back in. Taking that as her cue, she turned off the noise machine and walked to the screen room to tell them they could return.

"There you are! Are you ready for me?" Eva asked.

"As ready as I'm going to be."

They all trooped back to the living room where Reuben was still sitting on the floor and was grooming himself. He stopped mid-lick with his left hind leg up in the air and the tip of his tongue still showing. He quickly put his leg back down and assumed what he hoped was a haughty demeanor.

"Time for you to let us in on what you heard," Eva said and waited while he meowed Sarah's story to her. "Why, Sarah, I had no idea you had a wild side!" she teased when he had finished. She repeated the story for Vivian's benefit.

Don't blame the messenger for breaking the pact he added before jumping back up on his cushion in case there were repercussions between Vivian and Sarah.

Vivian's jaw had dropped, and she turned to Sarah wide-eyed. "We swore we'd never tell anyone about that." Her eyebrows were knit together and her eyes hard as she hissed out the words. The embarrassment of having the story told in front of Eva and Jim temporarily overshadowed the shock that Eva had learned it from a cat.

"And I never did until now. But that's the very reason why I chose that story. It's something we all shared and had sworn each other to secrecy."

Vivian's brows smoothed and she sighed. "Yeah, I can see your point." The words were barely out of her mouth when her jaw dropped a second time as the realization of how the disclosure of the story was possible hit her. She looked from Eva to Reuben and back again shaking her head, too stunned to speak.

"You don't have anything to worry about from us," Jim interjected, smiling. "It sounds like it was typical college break shenanigans. As far as skeletons in the closet go, that one isn't a reputation destroyer."

"No one will be hearing it from me, either." Eva pinched her thumb and forefinger together and ran them across her lips for emphasis.

"The reason I set up this demonstration wasn't just to prove that Eva can talk to animals. Our idea is to have her come to Meg's apartment after we make sure the bugs are gone. It's possible Panda saw or heard something that could give us a clue about who was in the apartment when Lily was killed."

Vivian nodded her head slowly, thinking over Sarah's plan.

"Now this makes more sense," she agreed. "Meghan might not be agreeable at first, but I think I can convince her to go along."

Sarah took a deep breath as though to summon her courage for what she was about to say.

"I told you all of us in the Club have different skills. Mine is that I can communicate with the dead. I'd like to try to speak to Lily. If you're okay with that, of course. I thought it would be best to speak to you first and have your permission before we mention it to Meghan. If you aren't on board with that idea, I'll respect your wishes."

Vivian blinked her eyes as they began to fill with tears.

"After what you just did with Reuben, I can't help but believe you're able to do that. Would... would I be able to see Lily or speak to her?"

"I honestly have no idea. Usually, I'm the only one who can do that, but we can try. It's also possible that she won't communicate with me at all."

Vivian nodded her head. "I understand, but I think we should do this."

"Okay. We should get going now. Hank Edwards is meeting us at the apartment to do the sweep."

Sarah had filled in Eva and Jim earlier about contacting Hank.

"Thank you for helping me with this," Sarah told Eva and Jim. They had been sitting quietly while she and Vivian discussed contacting Lily but now rose to walk them to the door. "We'll be back in touch when it looks safe for you to meet Panda."

"Yes, thank you, both," Vivian said and this time she was the one to hug first Eva and then Jim.

"My pleasure. Do we need to say what happens in Glen Lake stays in Glen Lake?" he joked.

Sarah glanced at Vivian to make sure she wasn't upset but was surprised to see a wide grin on her face as she winked at Jim.

Chapter 16

When Sarah and Vivian pulled into the nearly empty parking lot at the apartment building, they found Hank Edwards waiting in his car. He looked up from the tablet he was reading when Sarah parked in the empty spot next to his.

Hank was the first to step out of his car and walked to the rear hatch which he'd opened using the interior switch. Sarah introduced him to Vivian, whose first thought was *he doesn't look like someone who does this for a living*. She had been expecting someone who looked more like a Mission Impossible team member. Instead, Hank was a short man, no more than five feet six inches, if that. He was wearing a button-down shirt under his blue blazer and khaki pants; an outfit she would expect to see on a banker or insurance agent. He was completely bald, and wore black-frame glasses that shouted nerd rather than mirrored aviator-dangerous. He pulled an ordinary looking case from the back of his car.

So, not Mission Impossible, Vivian thought as she inspected the case in his hand. She wasn't sure how to take his serious expression but then he smiled, putting her more at ease.

"I've been told you need an exterminator," he addressed Vivian.

"That's what we're afraid of. I'm not sure if I'll be more relieved if you find bugs or you don't."

"Hey, Sarah. Good to see you again!"

"You, too, Hank. Thank you for coming out so quickly. We'd like to have this taken care of as soon as possible, so we really appreciate it."

"Have you decided if you want the bugs removed or should I leave them where I find them?"

Sarah and Vivian had already discussed what to say if Hank asked. There wasn't any reason to explain that they didn't want anyone listening while Eva had a conversation with Panda or that Sarah would be attempting to communicate with Lily. Even though both conversations would be one-sided to anyone listening, they weren't going to take any chances. Not to mention that there was no need for Sarah to risk her credibility with Hank thinking she had gone off the deep end. It was enough to leave the reason as being for Meghan's comfort.

"We'd like them removed," Vivian answered. "We realize it will probably tip off whoever put them there, but Meghan doesn't want to constantly worry about what she says. I'm just visiting but she'll be living here by herself when I'm gone."

"Can't say that I blame her. When we get into the apartment, I'm not going to say anything. The two of you can either wait out here or come in with me but if you do, remember not to make any comments about what I'm doing or acknowledge if I find any devices. I'll disable it and maybe they'll think it's stopped working because it's defective."

"Gotcha," Sarah replied.

They took the stairs up to the second floor with Vivian leading the way. As soon as she opened the door, Panda came running out to greet them. When he spotted Hank, he tried but couldn't stop his forward momentum and his back end skidded on the wood flooring. Scrabbling to regain his footing, he turned and ran back to the bedrooms and safety under a bed.

"We probably won't see him again for a while," Vivian said to Sarah, chuckling and then covered her mouth.

"He'll be okay. I think we must have surprised him," Sarah said. She nodded her head and gave Vivian a reassuring look that it was alright she'd spoken.

Hank mimed that he was going to begin his search and removed his equipment from the case.

"There's a new documentary about the national parks I've been wanting to see. Would you like to watch it?" Vivian asked.

Sarah frowned, not understanding at first what Vivian was doing but then had her aha moment. Turning on the television would create background noise and it wouldn't be obvious that they weren't talking if they were watching a program, on the chance that anyone was listening in.

"Yeah, sounds good."

Vivian switched on the television and queued up the program, turning the volume up higher than usual.

Hank gave them both a thumbs up realizing what they were doing and then began his sweep of the apartment. He started in the bedrooms and moved on to the kitchen before returning to the living room. He held up two devices for them to see and put his finger on his lips to signify he hadn't finished. They watched as he made his way around the room with no results until he swept over the lamp beside the couch and got a hit. Turning it upside down, he found the listening device on the base of the lamp. He took several photos of the lamp, the room, and the bug still installed on the lamp before he removed it. He swept the rest of the room, but he only had the three devices by the time he finished. He didn't speak until he removed their batteries and put them into his case and removed the latex gloves he was wearing before he closed the lid.

"That should do it. I took photos of the others, too. If whoever planted these left are any fingerprints on them, it will connect them to being here."

Vivian picked up the remote and turned off the television.

"Are you sure you don't want to give those to the police?" he asked Sarah.

"Not yet, but would you hold them for me? We may want to do that later."

"Can do. Should I send the bill to you?"

"No," Vivian interrupted. "Send it to me."

He handed her his phone. "You can put your contact information in here."

"That just made me think of something. Could they have tapped our phones remotely?" Vivian asked.

"Yes. If they have hacking skills or know someone who does, they could tap into the phones."

"Is there a way to know for sure?"

"If you've noticed the phone acting up, like hearing unusual sounds on calls, your battery drains or overheats, and there's a few more ways but you can check them by dialing special code numbers. There are different ones for Androids and iPhones. I'll write them down for you now in case you want to keep monitoring them until things settle down. You should also shut your phone off every day. That disconnects the tap." He took out two business cards and wrote the numbers on the back, handing one to Vivian and the other to Sarah. "It's been a pleasure, ladies. I'll show myself out." He picked up his case and took a few steps before turning to face them. "I almost forgot. Your cat is under the bed in the back bedroom. I may have scared him even more. He tucked himself up as far away from me as he could get." Giving them one last wave, he turned and walked out.

"What now?" Vivian asked.

"First, try that code. It's probably not necessary, but I'll do the same. If everything's copacetic, we call Eva. For now, though, I need to get back to work."

"I can't thank you enough, Sarah. I wouldn't have had a clue how to do this without you."

"Glad I can help. Have Meghan give me a call when she gets home from work so we can set up a time for Eva and me to come over. And tell her to turn her phone off for a few minutes. You can tell her about the codes when she gets home, and you can do it face-to-face. I think we should start doing this on a daily basis in case they figure it out and hack in again."

Chapter 17

"How did it go?" Ashley asked when Sarah returned home. "I should have gone into the office instead of trying to work from home. I haven't been able to concentrate all morning. All I can think about is how Vivian reacted and whether there were any bugs at their apartment."

Before Sarah could answer, Max bounded down the stairs and jumped up to greet her, nearly knocking her over in his enthusiasm.

"Down, boy. No jumping," she admonished but ruffled the fur at his neck and around his ears.

"You know you're just encouraging him by doing that."

"I do. But who can resist this shweet face," Sarah said, her words coming out in dog-speak and her face taking on the expression humans use when giving their dog love.

The smile on Max's face and the adoration in his eyes as he looked at Sarah confirmed he couldn't agree more with her assessment.

"Mmmmm, something smells good." The aroma of a stew caught Sarah's attention as she sat on the couch with Ashley. Max jumped up to his usual spot between them, circling twice before settling down with his chin on his front paws.

"The *bugs?*"

"Right, right. Hank found three. I told him to keep them in case we need to take them to police later. Now that I think of it, if Phil and Dennis agree to help us, we could hand them over to them for safekeeping."

"Wouldn't that be a problem if they had to take them in as evidence? The point of not doing that now was because you can't trust anyone else," Ashley reminded her.

"Good point! I'm glad I've got you to rein me in when I go off-track."

Max suddenly leapt up and ran to the door barking furiously, alarming both of the women. Sarah walked to the door and moved aside the curtain covering the window on the upper half just enough that she could glimpse outside. The covered front porch was faced with windows and the exterior door was completely glass allowing her a view of the sidewalk and street. There was no one at the door but although Max had stopped barking, he continued to growl menacingly beside her.

"There's no one out there, boy. Oh, wait, I see what got you all riled up," she said as she caught movement out of the corner of her eye. A man dressed all in black and wearing a baseball cap that was pulled down hiding his face strode out of their driveway and back to the sidewalk where he picked up his pace.

"Who are you and what are you doing in my driveway?" Sarah asked quietly, the question rhetorical.

Disregarding Ashley's protestation to stay inside, Sarah swung open the door and Max shoved his way past her and began barking again in earnest. She remained on the porch so that Max wouldn't bolt out to the sidewalk and stared at the back of the man who had already crossed the street and was now opening the driver's side door of a dark sedan three houses down from her. He suddenly turned around and Sarah knew he saw her but there was nowhere to hide. She tried her best to make out the details of his face, but the cap hid his features. He turned back and slid into the car and pulled away. The license plate had been partially obscured with dirt, but she was able to make out the numbers six and eight. She pulled on Max's collar to bring him back inside with her as a tingle of fear crept up her body.

Chapter 18

"Who was it?" Ashley asked.

"I don't know. It was a man. He was wearing a baseball cap and had it pulled down, so I couldn't see his face. But I have a feeling this is connected to Lily and Meghan."

"What was he doing?"

"He was walking out of the driveway, but our cars are in the garage, and I don't think there's any way he could have gotten inside without us hearing the door open."

"Why would he be here?"

Sarah struggled internally about her response when she heard the fear in Ashley's voice. *Might as well be honest. She'll know if you're lying so she won't worry.*

"The only thing I can think of is that he saw me with Meghan and Vivian earlier and followed me home today. We'll need to be extra careful about putting on the alarm when we leave the house… at least until this is over and Lily's killer is caught."

Sarah considered adding *and even when we're here* but decided against it. Ashley looked worried enough; no sense making it worse.

"I don't think we need to worry about him coming back

tonight, though. I'm probably just being paranoid, but Hank gave me codes to check our phones to see if they're tapped and I think we should check yours."

Ashley gave Sarah a long, assessing look but then nodded and handed over her phone. Sarah entered the codes and breathed a sigh of relief when no tap was detected.

Hoping to end any further speculation about being in danger, Sarah switched topics. "That stew is reminding me that I missed lunch today. How about we have an early dinner?"

"Come on, Max, let's get you some dinner, too," she said, and he happily trotted behind her to the kitchen.

Sarah held back to take out her phone and send a group text to the Club.

> Something's happened. We need to talk to Phil and Dennis right away.

Chapter 19

The mood was somber as Sarah recounted the details of her visit from the stranger exiting her driveway the night before. The group was gathered at Eva's dining room awaiting the arrival of Detectives Dennis Smith and Phil Roberts, which Jennifer had arranged earlier that day. Intentionally missing were Meghan and Vivian. They had decided to wait until their initial meeting with the detectives before bringing them in the loop. No one spoke when Sarah finished, each of them lost in their own thoughts about the encounter.

"Are you going to tell Phil and Dennis about the bugs?" Eva asked.

"That was my first thought, but it occurred to me that it might not be a good idea. I don't know if this is true or just Hollywood's version, but if they knew about it but didn't ask me to turn them over so they could put them into Evidence, it might be seen as withholding evidence in a crime. Not to mention that if they did turn them in, how would they explain how they got them since they're not part of the official investigation? And, who's to say the dirty cop wouldn't make them disappear? I think it's better for now if we leave them with Hank and say nothing."

"I hadn't thought of that, but I see your point," Eva said, and the others nodded their agreement.

"While we're on the subject of bugs, Hank told me how to check our phones to see if they're being tapped. This is probably overkill but better safe than sorry." Everyone pulled out their phones and Sarah gave them the instructions. The relief in the room was palpable when they finished and none of their phones was affected.

Before anyone had a chance to start the conversation rolling again, the doorbell rang.

"That must be them," Eva said, standing up to answer the door.

I thought Annalise was the psychic Reuben drawled in his dry tone.

Eva sent him a scathing glance and Reuben retreated to his cushion out of the line of fire, realizing she wasn't in the mood for teasing.

"We're all in the dining room," Eva announced after letting the detectives in, and gesturing the direction they should go.

Once seated, the ladies looked from one to another to see who would be the first to speak.

"I guess I'm the one who should get this started," Sarah said. She told them the order of events beginning with Meghan's call about Lily's death, the envelope Lily left for Vivian, Lily's role as a confidential informant for Mike Nicholson, the agent at the DEA, and ended with her description of the man who had been in her driveway the night before.

"Even though you're not assigned to this case, we were hoping you could help. We don't think Detective Brooks is bothering to investigate any other suspects and is focusing on Meghan."

Phil and Dennis nodded in agreement.

"I wish I could tell you I think you're wrong," Phil Roberts began, "but Brooks has a reputation for not being thorough.

He probably got assigned to this case because it looked like an accidental death at first, not a murder. There must have been something in the coroner's report indicating it wasn't or he would have closed the case immediately."

"He likes to have cases that can be wrapped up in a bow with as little legwork and paperwork as possible," Dennis Smith added.

"That's the impression we got, too," Sarah said. "We haven't told him about the envelope Lily left. After the warning in Lily's letter, we couldn't be sure if we could trust him. But we trust you. Do you think you can help us?"

The detectives exchanged glances and nodded their heads.

"We'll have to do this on the QT, but we'll do what we can. Everyone should get the justice they deserve, and we believe all suspects should be considered innocent until proven guilty. It's the duty of the officers to investigate all leads, not just the easy ones," Dennis said, and Phil nodded his head in agreement.

"And the last thing our department needs is a dirty cop," Phil said.

"Have you been able to reach the DEA agent Lily was working with?" Dennis asked.

"No, he's still on vacation as far as we know. Vivian didn't leave a message when she tried calling him and got the voice mail greeting. Do you know him?" Sarah asked.

"I haven't ever worked with him," Phil said and turned to Dennis.

"Me, either. I might have another contact there, though."

"You said you made copies of the journal and the recordings from the USB drives?" Dennis asked Sarah.

"Yes, I have them stored on a secure Cloud server. I also have the key that was in the envelope. We don't have a clue what it goes to, though. I brought it with me in case anyone had any ideas."

"Let me take a look," Jennifer offered. "Maybe I can get an impression from it."

"That's a great idea, Jennifer!" Eva said.

Sarah took an envelope with the key from her purse and handed it to Jennifer.

The atmosphere in the room became charged as she placed the key in her hand and curled her fingers around it. She closed her eyes and took several deep breaths to center herself.

Images began to appear in her mind's eye. She was standing in front of a commercial building. Opening the door, she walked into a lobby where the only sound was her footsteps on the tile flooring. All around her were rows of gray metal enclosures fronted by doors with padlocks. She walked to the last aisle. She hesitated, deciding which way to go, and was drawn to the second unit. Glancing up, she saw the number 89 written in black and slipped the key into the padlock and turned it. She heard the click of the lock releasing and pulled on the curved bar to swing it open enough that she could remove the padlock. The image of the padlock disappeared, and the scene switched to the exterior of the building. Her eyes focused on the sign attached to the building: CITY U-STORE 207-555-9000.

Jennifer's eyes fluttered several times before opening them.

"Did you see anything?" Annalise asked.

Jennifer smiled. "I did and I think you're going to be excited."

Chapter 20

The members of the Club had witnessed Jennifer's skills of psychometry before, but this was a first for the detectives. They knew of her ability but hadn't seen it in action first-hand.

If someone told me two months ago I'd be sitting here waiting to find out what some woman claimed she was seeing in a vision while she's holding onto a key, I would have told them they were full of it, Dennis was thinking.

When she finished recounting what she had seen, Dennis Smith took out his cell phone and looked up CITY U-STORE.

"Here it is. You're right about the phone number. There's only one location and it's on the lower end of Main Street."

"Were you able to see anything that might be inside?" Eva asked.

Jennifer shook her head. "No, the scene changed too fast. I think it was more important for me to see where it was located and that we're meant to go there ourselves."

"We should tell Vivian. Technically, this belongs to her now," Sarah said.

"It must be connected to the drug ring, don't you think?

Why else would Lily have kept it inside the envelope with the journal and drives?" Eva asked.

"It might be better to wait until you've made contact with the DEA agent," Dennis cautioned. "These people are dangerous, and you don't know what you'd be getting into. It might be best to leave it to the professionals."

Sarah nodded her head and then a look of alarm came over her face. "They could have put two and two together from when they were listening in and figured out how I'm connected. If it wasn't just me being paranoid, that guy must have come to my house looking for the copies of the journal and the recordings or he was doing reconnaissance. He probably figured no one would be home during the day. If he comes back again and breaks in and one of us is there alone…"

"Do you have a security system in your house?" Phil asked.

"We do, and I don't mean Max." The ladies laughed but the detectives looked confused.

"Max is our golden retriever," Sarah explained for their benefit. "I don't remember if Meghan or Vivian mentioned finding the key in Lily's envelope before the bugs were removed. We're only guessing it's related somehow because it was in the envelope, but it's probably not a good idea to take the key home with me just in case they're looking for it. Would you mind if I left it here, Eva?"

"Of course! It's not likely they'd come to my house, unless you think you were being followed here?"

"That hadn't occurred to me, but I don't think so. I don't want you to feel like you have to do this, or put you in any danger,"

"What if I take it with me?" Annalise offered. "I have a security system, too. It should be safe there."

With that settled and nothing else to add to what they'd told the detectives, they called it a night.

"We'll follow you home to make sure you get there safely," Dennis told Sarah as they were leaving.

Her knee-jerk reaction was to protest that it wasn't necessary, but after what had happened and not knowing for sure if she was being followed, she reconsidered. She hadn't realized how anxious she was until she noticed how reassuring it was to see their headlights behind her on the drive home. After she checked to make sure all was well, she turned to wave at them and they pulled away. Her shoulders dropped from the spot below her ears where they'd been during the drive home as the tension she'd been holding onto released.

"What's up?" Ashley asked, her eyes scrunched as she watched Sarah.

"Phil and Dennis followed me home to make sure I got here safely. We'll need to remember to activate the alarm for a while." Sarah caught Ashley's eyes widening. "It's only a precaution until they catch Lily's killer. It shouldn't be for long," Sarah said. *I hope* she thought, hoping her tone had sounded more confident to Ashley than it did to herself.

Chapter 21

"So, how does this work, exactly?" Meghan asked. "Do we sit around a table holding hands? Do I need to light some candles?"

Eva and Sarah were at her apartment, seated in the living room along with Vivian. There was an air of anticipation mixed with nervousness on Meghan and Vivian's part.

Sarah laughed. "Well, you can if you want to but, no, it's not like in the movies when they're having a séance. Eva and I talked about this on our way over and agreed it would be best for her to stay with Panda in one of the bedrooms and I'll go to the kitchen to try to make contact with Lily. You're welcome to stay here or join me there. You probably won't be able to see or hear Lily but if you have something you'd like to say to her, I'll let you know when it's a good time. I'd like to find out what happened the day she was killed first, though. That's the main reason we're doing this, and I don't have control over how much time we'll have."

Vivian's face fell and her shoulders sank, but she nodded to acknowledge she understood. "I'd like to be with you and please tell me if it's okay to speak."

"I'd like that, too," Meghan said. "If you don't think

there's going to be much time, could you tell Lily how sorry I am. I haven't been able to stop thinking that if I'd only let her explain, she wouldn't..." She had to stop as the sobs welled up and she was unable to continue.

"You can't blame yourself, Meghan. I don't," Vivian told her. "Lily was involved in some dangerous stuff and if there's anybody I blame, it's the DEA agent for putting her in the position he did. And then to go off on vacation? How could he do that and not think that she could get hurt?"

Meghan took a tissue from the box on the coffee table and blew her nose.

"Thank you for that. I've been so worried even though you haven't said anything, and you haven't seemed angry."

"You should have said something sooner. We could have talked it through."

"I think I was afraid to bring it up."

"Oh, come here," Vivian said and took Meghan in her arms.

Sarah and Eva waited silently while Vivian comforted Meghan, knowing they both needed to make that connection. When Meghan resumed control of her emotions, she addressed them.

"Maybe we should begin now. I'll take you back to meet Panda, Eva. He might try to crawl under the bed if you go in alone."

They walked to Meghan's bedroom, and she shut the door softly behind them to make sure Panda didn't run out when he saw Eva. Eva surveyed the room which tastefully decorated in coordinating shades of blue, looking for the best spot for her and Panda. Meghan's queen size bed was to the right of the door, centered on the back wall. A desk with her laptop and other work-related supplies faced the windows which looked down on the street in front of the apartment building on the opposite wall from the bed. A bureau was placed on the long, windowless wall directly opposite the door leading into the bedroom, which Eva guessed must abut the apartment next to it. They found Panda curled up on her bed in front of a mound of pillows which leaned up against the headboard.

Panda raised his head blinking the sleep from his eyes before coming to full alert status when he spotted Eva. He quickly rolled over to stand on all four legs, but Meghan picked him up in her arms before he could jump off the bed. She had to hold tighter as he struggled to free himself.

"It's alright, Panda. Eva isn't going to hurt you. She's here to talk to you about the night Lily was killed."

Panda's ears were flattened to his head, and he was emitting a low growl from his throat.

What is the point of that? It's not like she can understand me.

"It's okay, baby. I know you're scared but it's okay. And, yes, I can understand you. That *is* the point of why I'm here."

Eva reiterated what Panda had said for Meghan's and Panda's benefit. When he heard his words repeated verbatim, he stopped struggling, too shocked to move.

"That's right. I can communicate with most animals although cats and dogs are easiest. I have a cat named Reuben who gives me sass every day, but we enjoy the banter. I'm sorry that what I have to ask you is going to be difficult to relive, but my friends and I… and Meghan… are trying to find the person who hurt Lily so they can be arrested. Can you tell me what you remember about what happened?"

At first Panda was silent, and Eva gave him the time to process what was happening. Meghan sat down with him on the bed and stroked his head, trying to calm him. When she felt his body relax, she loosened her grip, and he stayed in her lap.

"That's a good boy. I'm right here. You don't have to be afraid," she cooed.

Eva thought about sitting on the bed with them but

decided against it. Instead, she took the chair that was at the desk and brought it over to the end of the bed.

"This is very important, Panda. If you saw anything that night, it would be a big help to hear what it was."

I was asleep on the couch. Meghan and Lily had been fighting so I was staying out of their way. Meghan left but not long after that, someone knocked at the door and Lily let them in. I heard the voices of two men, but I couldn't see their faces from where I was sitting. I could tell they weren't nice men, though. Their voices were angry.

"Did Lily call either of them by name?"

She called one of them Randy. He called the other one Boss, but Lily never said his name.

"Thank you, Panda. That is very helpful. You said you couldn't see them when they first came into the apartment, but did you get a look at them later?"

Their voices were getting angrier, and it scared me. I decided to hide in the bedroom under Meghan's bed and was creeping past the kitchen so they wouldn't see me. Right as I got there, one of the men grabbed Lily and told her she better hand over the journal and the recordings or else. I saw his face when they were fighting. He was taller than Lily. The other man was about the same height as the one who was grabbing Lily. I think he was a policeman. He wasn't wearing a uniform, but he had to move to get out of their way and I saw a badge on his belt, and he had a gun under his arm. I think there was a strap over his shoulder with a bag that the gun was in. They were under his jacket, so I didn't see them at first, but his jacket opened up. That's when I saw them.

"That's very good information, Panda. Is there anything else you can tell me?" Even though he used the word bag, she recognized his description as a shoulder holster.

The man who was fighting with Lily was wearing a hat. It was blue and had something on the front. It looked like a star and a picture of a man but there was a long tail coming out of the back of his head.

Eva frowned as she tried to imagine what Panda was describing. It wasn't coming to her, but perhaps when she told the others, they could identify it.

The bad man hurt Lily. They knocked over everything that was on the table when she tried to get away and then she got loose but she fell backwards and hit her head on the counter. She fell to the floor and then she didn't move. The bad men turned around and I ran back into the living room to hide under the couch but they didn't come after me. I could hear them moving around and crawled out far enough that I could see what they were doing. They picked up the lamp and put something on the bottom of it and then they went into the bedrooms. I stayed under the couch. After a couple minutes, they opened the door and I ran out past them.

"I'm so sorry, Panda," Eva said, her voice gentle. "That must have been very scary for you."

Meghan had remained quiet during their conversation. Although she couldn't understand Panda's side of it, she got the gist, and nuzzled her face against his neck.

"I think that's enough for now," Eva told Meghan. "We can go back to the living room, and I'll fill you all in when Sarah is done."

Meghan left Panda on the bed and joined Eva. Before leaving the bedroom, she looked back and saw him curled up in a ball. Their eyes met and Meghan could swear she could see sadness in his eyes. "I'm sorry you had to go through all that, baby. You're safe now," she said softly.

Chapter 22

Vivian and Sarah looked up expectantly when Eva and Meghan returned, curiosity showing on both their faces.

"Panda was able to tell me what happened, but I'd like to write it down while it's fresh in my mind and we'll have it for later. Why don't I do that while you try to contact Lily, Sarah?" She went to her purse and pulled out a small notebook and pen.

Vivian's face registered her disappointment at having to wait, but she didn't object.

"Would you two like to come with me?" Sarah asked.

Vivian and Meghan nodded their agreement and followed her as far as the cased opening of the kitchen, but then stood at the entrance unsure of whether they should come in.

"It's okay for you to sit at the table so you'll be more comfortable," Sarah told them when she noticed their hesitation. "I'll need a couple minutes to center myself and like I said earlier, please just wait quietly until I say it's okay to speak."

Their heads nodded in unison. There was an air of pins and needles in the room as they took seats at the table.

Meghan clasped her hands together tightly on the table and Vivian sat on the edge of her chair.

Sarah remained standing and closed her eyes. The only sound in the room was the ticking of the clock hanging on the wall above the table. Sarah's breaths stretched out as she inhaled deeply and exhaled slowly until at last, she opened her eyes.

"Hello, Lily." She turned to Meghan and Vivian and then back to the spot where her eyes had been focused. "We're all here to find out what happened the night you were killed. We hope it will help us find your killer so they can be arrested."

Meghan and I had a fight when she found out I was dealing drugs, but she didn't understand what was really going on.

"She does now. Vivian got your envelope from the safe deposit box. They're both sorry they misjudged you."

I can see that, she said looking in their direction. *Please tell them I forgive them.*

"Lily asked me to tell you she forgives you both," Sarah said, but kept her eyes on Lily.

It was only a few minutes after Meghan left to cool off that I had a knock on the door. It was Randy Hughes, the man who I got the drugs from and another man. I'd only seen him once before and I don't know what his name was. Randy didn't introduce him, and he only called him Boss. They'd found out somehow that I was keeping a journal and recordings of my meetings with Randy and they wanted me to turn them over to them. I tried to tell them I couldn't do that because I'd given them to my sister who lives out-of-state, but I wouldn't give them her name. Randy grabbed me and was threatening me so I would tell him. We were struggling and I got loose but I lost my balance and fell back-wards. I think I hit my head on the countertop of the island. The next thing I knew, I felt myself leaving my body and I was looking down on them... and me. I knew that I had died and as soon as they realized I was dead, they put a bug here in the kitchen, another one under the lamp in the living room, and one more in my bedroom. Randy knew which one was mine because he'd followed me in there another time when he'd been to the apartment. Then they left and Meghan found me when she got back.

"Can you describe them for us, Lily?"

She repeated the same description Panda had given Eva.

"I almost forgot; can you tell us about the key that was in the envelope?"

It goes to a storage unit at U-STORE STORAGE on Main Street. Number 89. Randy needed something out of it the week before and didn't have time to go himself, so he told me to. He trusted me then. He must have found out about the journal afterwards. I made a copy of the key he gave me to give to Mike Nicholson. He's the DEA agent I was working with… or more like the one I was working for since I was just a confidential informant to him.

Lily's tone had taken on an edge of bitterness when she spoke about the agent.

I wouldn't be dead if I hadn't been doing their dirty work.

"I can understand how you would feel that way," Sarah said. "Is there anything in the storage unit that would help the police arrest Randy?"

You can't trust the police! Lily said emphatically and with a sense of urgency.

"We are working with two homicide detectives we can trust. They've agreed to help us catch your killer."

He didn't really kill me, though. I lost my balance.

Sarah was surprised at first by Lily's defense of Randy but then understood her logic. "I see your point, but I think he could be guilty of manslaughter. He didn't even bother to get help for you by calling 911. It might not have saved you, but he could at least have tried even if it was with an anonymous phone call."

Lily considered Sarah's words and then nodded her head.

That part doesn't matter now. It's too late. But if you can help get him and his boss arrested, maybe that would help someone else.

"Is there anything else you can tell me?"

Not about that night but can you tell Vivian I love her? And Meghan, too? There's nothing they could have done to stop it from happening. They need to get in touch with Mike and take the recordings to him. There are two he hasn't heard before and on one of them, I was able to record the boss talking to Randy. Maybe it could be used to identify him. Mike went on vacation right before I recorded it.

"I'll do that but first, Vivian would like to speak to you if you are okay with that?"

Lily nodded her head and Sarah turned to Vivian. "You can talk to Lily now."

"This is so weird," Vivian began, feeling self-conscious and a little embarrassed about speaking to nothing but air. Remembering Sarah's caution that Lily's time might be short, she found her resolve to speak. "Lily, I'm so sorry I judged you about the drugs and that I wasted so much time not being with you when I had the chance. I was disappointed with you thinking you were doing something that could put you in jail and you wouldn't listen to me when I told you that you should stop. I understand now, but it's too late and I'll regret it until the day I die." Her voice caught in her throat making it difficult to continue. "I think that's all I needed to say," she told Sarah when she was able to speak again.

"I just want to say I feel the same as Vivian. I didn't know what was going on for as long as she did, but I wish I had given you the chance to defend yourself. I thought we had time… and now we never will. I'm sorry," Meghan said once Vivian was done.

Please tell them I forgive them. I think they need to hear it again. And I love them.

Sarah repeated Lily's words for Vivian and Meghan and when she turned back to where Lily had been, she was gone.

Chapter 23

The Club was gathered around Eva's dining room table enjoying their dessert before beginning their sewing session for the week's meeting.

"That was one of our better potluck dinners, but I could hardly concentrate on it. I've been dying to ask but contained myself until now. So, spill the tea, what happened with Panda and Lily?" Annalise asked.

"Me, too!" Jennifer agreed.

"Is it horrible of me to admit that I've been holding back just to see how long it would take you to ask?" Sarah asked, a mischievous expression on her face.

"Yes!" Jennifer and Annalise said in unison. They both were smiling so Sarah knew there were no hard feelings.

"Do you want to go first, Eva?'

Eva held up her index finger and finished her bite of chocolate cake before responding.

"That was the first time I've had flourless chocolate cake, but it's not going to be the last. I'm not sure if I should thank you or curse you for bringing it, Jennifer."

"You're welcome," Jennifer said, grinning.

"Here's what happened." Eva recited her conversation with Panda as Jennifer and Annalise listened.

"Did that match any of what Lily told you?" Jennifer asked.

"It did and Lily was able to tell us more about the men who were there that night. And she confirmed what you saw about the storage unit, Jennifer." Sarah told them about the rest of her conversation with Lily.

"Do you think it might have been the DEA agent who tipped them off? How else would the drug dealers have found out about the envelope if they didn't bug the apartment until the night Lily was killed?" Annalise asked.

"I've been wondering that same thing. If we can't trust the police or the DEA, where does that leave us?"

Chapter 24

They were silent as they each considered how they could proceed.

"We should tell Phil and Dennis what we've learned. We don't have to worry that they're the type of cops who would take a bribe. Maybe they have someone they trust who could check out Mike Nicholson. It's always bothered me that he went on vacation at the same time that all this happened," Eva said, breaking the silence.

"I agree," Jennifer said. "I think we should suggest to Vivian that she wait until they can tell us if it's safe to get in touch with the DEA. If they can, of course. It's still risky. How would they know for sure if he is on the take? If he was, wouldn't the DEA have fired or arrested him by now?"

"That's a good point, too," Sarah said.

The four women sat quietly again, glum expressions reflecting the mood.

"We're not going to get any answers until we can talk to Dennis and Phil," Eva said at last. "Why don't we table that for tonight and move on to our projects." After they all settled at their stations in Eva's sewing room, she asked. "How is your banner coming along, Sarah?"

"Not bad! I haven't made as much progress as I would have liked but there have been a few interruptions in my routine this week." Her wry expression elicited sympathetic nods as everyone empathized with her situation. "I was torn about the color for the spider web. Part of me thought I should make it white to be more realistic, but it felt too drab, so I went to Quilting Essentials and asked Evelyn for help. She suggested using shades of orange so that's what I'm using. It's more Halloween-ie. And, yes, that is a word even if I did make it up," Sarah declared.

"No argument from me. Halloween-ie it is!" Annalise said, smiling. "I decided to go with a spider web in one corner and pumpkins on the bottom. I wanted to try appliquéing them on. It's so much easier with that technique." She held up her work in progress for everyone to see. "I did go with white for the spider's web but it still shows up on the blue background for the sky section. I'm really happy with how the pumpkin patch turned out. The appliqués are all attached and tonight I'm going to stitch around the edges with the blanket stitch setting on my sewing machine."

"One of the things I love about quilting is how similar projects can turn out so differently simply by switching out the fabric choices. Mine is the same pattern as Sarah's but I'm making it scrappy. I'm very proud of myself that I used fabrics from my stash for a change." Jennifer held her project up for inspection.

"That leaves me. I'm not sure if my project is inspired or lazy," Eva said, smiling. "I decided I could make the whole thing as one giant spider web and that's it for the design. I used a plain white background and for the *webbing*? There's probably a name for the threads that make the web sections, but I'd have to google it. Anyway, this is the second lazy part. I decided to use quarter inch black iron on bias tape to create the web design and I'll use that as the guides for my quilting. Plus, it will keep the tape in place which I have a problem with sometimes. What do you think?" she asked as she showed them her project.

Sarah groaned as she facepalmed. "Why didn't I think of that? My pattern calls for using that bias tape to make the web design, but it never occurred to me to just put it on a white background."

"True confession. I got the idea when I was looking at your pattern," Eva confessed.

"I'll go with inspired, not lazy, Eva. I never would have thought of doing that either; and yet it's such an obvious way to construct it when you see it," Annalise said.

"It doesn't matter if it's inspired or lazy, I love it, Eva. And who couldn't use a hack like that to whip something up if they don't have the time for a more involved project?" Jennifer said.

"Thank you. And on that note, it's time to wrap things up for tonight as far as the sewing goes. What are we going to do about the Lily situation?"

Jennifer was the first to volunteer. "I'll give the detectives a call tomorrow. I'll send a group text when I hear back. We should probably set up an in-person meeting if that works for all of you," she suggested and all three nodded their assent.

Chapter 25

The Club met at Sarah's house along with Meghan and Vivian. Max began to bark and ran to the door when he heard the sound of footsteps at the front porch.

"That must be Phil and Dennis," Sarah said, reaching the door at the same time as she heard their knock. "Settle down, Max." He was growling low in his throat and let out a short bark despite Sarah's warning. She put her fingers under his collar to keep him from jumping on them when she opened the door. "It's okay. He's loud but harmless," she told the detectives and Max proved her point by licking Phil's hand. Sarah observed a flicker of surprise come across their faces when they noticed Meghan and Vivian sitting on the couch, and she realized they had not met yet.

"Detectives, this is Meghan Doherty and Vivian Sullivan, Lily's sister," and then introduced Phil and Dennis for Meghan and Vivian's benefit. "We thought it best that they be included in this meeting, so everyone is on the same page. Oh, and one other tiny thing. We found out who was in Lily's apartment when she died."

Phil groaned as he dropped his chin on his chest.

Dennis gave him a side-eye, but Phil remained quiet. He

sighed and squared his shoulders. "I'm going to regret this, but I'll ask anyway. How do you know who it was?"

Eva and Sarah repeated their discoveries from their conversations with Panda and Lily while the detectives listened intently and without judgement or disbelief. The ladies had proven themselves to be telling the truth about their paranormal skills on several occasions. Even so, it's not something they would share with their fellow officers, knowing they would be laughed out of the room. "Obviously, there's no way we can report what we've learned about Randy Hughes and his boss."

"We're also concerned that the leak about the journals came from the agent Lily was working with as his CI. If we turn over the evidence Lily collected, it could be falling into the wrong hands. Do you know anyone you can trust to ask about him without tipping him off?" Vivian asked.

"I might have someone," Phil said. "Do you remember Nick Talbot? We worked with him on the Nelson case," he asked Dennis.

"Now that you mention it, yeah, I do remember him. I think he could be trusted."

"I'll get in touch with him as soon as possible," Phil addressed Vivian and then turned to Meghan. "Has Detective Brooks questioned you again?"

"No. I'm hoping that means he figured out I'm not guilty and is investigating other leads."

"I hope so, too. At least he hasn't arrested you. I admit I'm surprised he hasn't, but the case isn't a slam dunk. All he has is circumstantial evidence since you can't prove your alibi. I shouldn't speak negatively about a fellow officer, but he's lazy and takes the easy way out whenever he can," Phil said.

"I think he's been in court to testify on a couple other cases this past week. That kept him occupied," Dennis reminded Phil.

"I'd forgotten that. So much for giving him the benefit of

the doubt about doing investigative work," Phil said, with a wry smile.

The disdain they both had for Brooks couldn't have been more obvious.

Chapter 26

"I think we should go to the storage unit," Meghan said after the detectives left. "I didn't want to say anything while the detectives were here in case they tried to talk us out of it. Maybe there's something in there that would tie Randy Hughes and his boss to Lily."

"I don't know, Meg. That could be dangerous," Vivian cautioned, her forehead wrinkled.

"You should go," Annalise spoke up, surprising everyone. "And I'll go with you. It would be too much for all of us to be there but only one more should be okay. And I can keep lookout while the two of you look inside. Plus, I've got my psychic powers on our side," she added, smiling to lighten the tense mood when she saw the doubt on everyone's face. "I can tune in to my intuition to warn us if anyone's coming. And, if that's not enough to convince you, I had a vision earlier today telling me that there is something of Lily's inside. I think it's the envelope with her evidence. And…" she paused for dramatic effect. "I've got the key."

"Alright, I agree we should go. I just hope we don't regret it," Vivian conceded.

⸻

ANNALISE MET them the next day in the lobby of Meghan's apartment building.

"We should take my car," Annalise said when Meghan took her car keys out of her jacket pocket. "Randy Hughes and his boss won't recognize mine. If they even notice my car, they'll probably think it's just someone else who's there to get into their storage unit."

"Right. I didn't think of that. My nerves are a little on edge, so I'm glad you're thinking ahead," she told Annalise and put her keys back in her pocket.

Annalise studied Meghan's face. "Do you want to call this off?"

"No, no. I'll be fine. It's important that we find that evidence. You're sure it's there?"

"As sure as I can be. My visions don't always come true, but this one has that quality about it that I get when they do."

"That's good enough for me. Let's go," Vivian said, giving Meghan's arm a nudge.

Annalise turned into the empty parking lot at the U-STORE STORAGE facility ten minutes later.

"This is a good sign," she said. "We might be able to let ourselves in and out without anyone seeing us." She scanned the length of the roofline, but didn't see evidence of any security cameras. Looking around when they got inside, she didn't see any there either. *Makes sense. It's not likely that drug dealers would risk having a storage unit someplace where their activities would be recorded and possibly incriminate them,* she thought.

The building wasn't heated but it wasn't the cold that made Meghan shiver. Her nerves were stretched so tight, she thought they might snap, as they walked down the aisles to the back of the building, each of them checking the numbers of the units as they moved along.

"Could you see where we should look?" Vivian asked

Annalise when they finally reached unit 89. "It would save us some time so we could get in and out as quickly as possible if we didn't have to look through everything."

"I saw a file cabinet in the back right corner. They have a table set up in the middle of the space where they sort out and bag the pills to give to their dealers but it's not in the way," Annalise said. "I think one of you should take a video on your phone that we can show Phil and Dennis and the DEA agent if we find out he's not the leak. They wouldn't be able to use it in court, but we can prove we found what we're looking for in this unit. We can't take it with us or it would tip them off."

"I'll do it," Meghan offered. She took out her phone and set the camera app to video. She panned up to the number 89 for proof of the location of the storage unit and then back down to Vivian.

Vivian took a deep breath and inserted the key into the padlock. "Is everybody ready?" When Meghan and Annalise nodded their heads, she held her breath and turned the key. The lock made a soft clicking sound as the shackle released. She removed the lock from the hasp, handing it to Meghan who put it in her jacket pocket, and bent down to pull the door up. It opened faster than she expected and the metal on metal made a loud high-pitched screeching noise that made them all wince.

"I better go back to the end of the aisle where I can keep an eye on the door, and warn you if anyone comes in," Annalise said. "You might want to try closing that more slowly when we're done. If Hughes or his boss come in, they'll be far enough away when I see them that they won't suspect it's their unit, but better safe than sorry."

"I'm sorry. I wasn't expecting it to go up so easily," Vivian apologized.

"That's okay. You two better get started. Are you still recording?" Annalise asked.

"Mmm hmmm," Meghan replied after checking her phone to make sure.

"Good luck!" Annalise said and walked back to the corner, stepping as lightly as possible even though no one else was in the building.

Vivian pulled her phone out of the pocket in her jeans and clicked on the flashlight icon, illuminating the space. *Right on the money so far.* Exactly as Annalise had described, there was a table in the middle of the room. It was a white folding banquet table, probably eight feet in length. At first, they didn't notice the clear plastic bags filled with pills because they blended in.

Vivian pointed wordlessly at the table and Meghan understood she wanted her to record it.

On the perimeter of the unit were stacks of plastic bins that looked like they held clothing and items that would typically be in a storage unit.

Meghan shrugged her shoulders, scrunched her eyebrows, and turned out the palm of her hand that wasn't holding her phone in the universal body language of *what the heck?* at Vivian.

"They probably want to create the appearance that the space is actually being used as a regular storage unit instead of where they bag up their drugs. Keep videotaping all of it anyway," Vivian answered her.

The space was about fifteen feet in length from the door to the back wall. *Bingo!* Vivian thought and pointed to the corner on the right side where they saw the filing cabinet Annalise had told them would be there.

"What if it's locked?" Vivian asked Meghan, her voice panicked.

"There's only one way to find out. Try opening the drawer." Meghan kept her voice even to reassure Vivian but the butterflies in her stomach were not helping. "Wait a second until I move over here in front of you so I can see you better for the video."

"This looks good," she said once she found the optimal position. "I'm recording now."

Vivian tried the top drawer, and they were both relieved when it slid open. Instead of hanging file folders, the contents were stacked inside in a pile. Vivian took the pile out and walked to the table to sort through it and Meghan followed, standing beside her so she could catch it all for the video.

Vivian waited to sort through the pile and raised her eyebrows questioningly when Meghan looked ready.

Meghan nodded to give her the green light.

The first two items on the top of the stack were travel brochures. Vivian looked up at Meghan with a what the heck expression and then sucked in her breath when underneath the last brochure was Lily's envelope which was easily recognizable by Vivian's name written on the outside.

They heard Annalise's voice in the distance asking if they were almost done. Vivian replaced the pile as she'd found it and closed the cabinet drawer. Meghan nodded her head at Vivian to signal that she had checked the recording to make sure she had everything.

"We're all set," Meghan called out to Annalise when she and Vivian had returned to the front of the unit.

Annalise felt a tingle up her arms and turned her head back to the door. Her intuition of someone coming was confirmed when a car pulling into the lot came into view.

"Hurry up and get the door closed and locked. Someone's coming!" she called out as quietly as possible to warn them.

Meghan took the lock from her pocket and was about to put it back into the hasp.

"I can't find the key," Vivian's voice was frantic as she felt inside her jacket pockets and found them empty.

"*What do you mean, you can't find the key?*" Meghan hissed. "What if it's them? We'll get caught."

"Don't you think I know that?" Vivian's anger came from

a place of fear but in the moment, Meghan was shocked by its intensity. "Open the door. I must have dropped it inside. *Move!*" she emphasized when Meghan hesitated.

Don't pull it too hard, Meghan cautioned herself. She rolled the door back up slowly hoping to avoid repeating the loud screeching noise from the first time. Vivian already had her phone out and the flashlight on and Meghan took hers out, too.

"You take that side and I'll look over here," Vivian whispered.

They shone the lights on the floor as they walked inside on either side of the table. Meghan felt a nudge of intuition telling her to shine her light on the filing cabinet, and the glint of light on metal caught her eye.

"It's on top of the filing cabinet! You must have put it there when you took the stuff out. Go get it so we can get out of here. I'll start pulling the door down."

Vivian ran to the back of the unit, thankful that the floor was concrete instead of metal, and her footsteps wouldn't be as loud. She grabbed the key, jammed it in her jeans pocket and ran back to the doorway. Meghan had already pulled the door a third of the way down, forcing Vivian to duck under it.

What is taking them so long? Annalise thought and looked down the aisle to find no one there. *Where the he…* Before she had a chance to finish the thought, Meghan stepped out of the unit and began pulling down the door and Vivian ducked out after her.

"*Get that door down and locked!* There are two men coming to the door and I have a feeling it's the dealers," Annalise warned them again, coming partway down the aisle so she wouldn't have to shout and then ran back to the end of the aisle to keep watch.

She peeked around the corner of the aisle just as the men opened the door and walked in her direction. She pulled her head back out of their line of sight, closed her eyes, and took a deep breath to concentrate. In her mind's eye she saw them coming to the aisle they were in and turn toward unit 89. She opened her eyes. *Try not to make any noise but hurry!* Her heart raced as she walked briskly to where Meghan and Vivian were still standing and reached them just as Vivian was locking the padlock.

"We need to go out the other side. They're coming here the way we came in, but we have time to get to the door out of their sight if we leave now. *Don't run!* It will make more noise and they'll know we're here," she whispered as they listened, their eyes opened wide with fear.

They nodded their heads but Annalise recognized their deer-in-the-headlights reaction and they weren't moving. "Come on, get going!" As soon as she put her hands on them and gently pushed, it broke the spell and they both turned and walked to the end of the row of units with Annalise close behind them. Vivian was walking in front and abruptly stopped before reaching the next aisle's opening causing Meghan to nearly bump into her.

"Why are you stopping?" she brought her mouth up to Vivian's ear and whispered.

"I want to see around the corner to make sure we won't be passing the opening at the same time they are," Vivian whispered back.

"Oh! Got it," Meghan whispered as she processed what Vivian was thinking.

Vivian poked her head around the corner, waited a second, and then motioned with her hand that they could move on. They followed until she reached the next aisle and held her fist up. Meghan had to fight a fit of hysterical giggles thinking how they must look like a commando team in an action movie with Vivian taking point.

Don't laugh! Don't laugh! She put her hand over her mouth and bit her tongue gently, but with purpose, to help control herself.

They continued in this way until they reached the front door and slipped outside and jogged back to Annalise's car, making sure not to slam the doors. Annalise put the car in gear and drove out of the parking lot but stole a look in her rearview mirror. She saw the men coming out the door of the storage facility, but made the executive decision not to tell Meghan and Vivian. Relief flowed through her when their car turned in the opposite direction out of the parking lot and her white-knuckle grip on the steering wheel loosened.

In the backseat, Meghan fought the urge to giggle again. All the nervous energy she'd kept under control while they were in the storage facility threatened to escape. She pressed her hand against her mouth, but this time it didn't work and she began laughing uncontrollably out loud.

Vivian turned to look at her, her mouth open and her eyes wide with astonishment and Meghan saw Annalise looking at her in the rearview mirror. This only made her laugh harder, holding onto her stomach with both hands and leaning over.

"*What in the world is wrong with you?*" Vivian asked, scowling.

"I can't stop thinking about you... acting like a soldier taking point... holding your fist up..." Meghan gasped the words out in between bouts of laughter and held her own hand up, fist closed.

Vivian's eyebrows were knit together and she cocked her head to one side and stared at Meghan, but Annalise began laughing along with her.

"I couldn't believe it either. I had to bite the inside of my cheeks so I wouldn't laugh out loud," Annalise said.

Vivian looked from one to the other and then a wide grin broke across her face.

"We're regular Charlie's Angels," Meghan replied, wiping the tears rolling down her cheeks and began hooting with laughter again. This time Vivian joined them.

Chapter 27

The Club called another special session including Meghan and Vivian, to show Dennis Smith and Phil Roberts the recording of the storage unit. They were meeting at Eva's house this time in case Sarah's or Meghan's houses were being watched. Their jubilant mood was soon crushed when the detectives found out what they had done. Rather than praising them for finding the evidence that linked the dealers to Lily, they got a lecture.

"Do you realize how much danger you put yourselves in?" Phil Robertson's voice was stern.

Meghan, Vivian, and Annalise exchanged glances, all of them silently sharing their relief that they hadn't mentioned the part about how close they had come to being caught when the dealers came to the storage facility.

"But we weren't," Vivian said, her tone defiant. "Obviously you can't use the video as evidence, but it proves they were involved with Lily."

"She has a point, Phil," Dennis said.

Phil glowered at Dennis, annoyed that he wasn't backing him up.

"If it has both of their fingerprints on the envelope,

couldn't you use that to find out who the other guy is?" Meghan asked.

"We'd have to have the envelope first and, as you pointed out, it's not like we have cause to get a search warrant and put it into evidence," Phil replied. "Or even put in a request for running the request for fingerprint ID without a case number, for that matter." He was still scowling, and the tension in the room was palpable.

Annalise spoke up to try to break the mood. "You're right. We probably shouldn't... "

"Not probably, *definitely*," Phil growled.

"Okay, definitely," Annalise conceded, "but we did and now we have more information than we did before. How about you? Were you able to find out anything about the DEA agent?"

Dennis stepped in this time to give Phil a few minutes to cool off.

"We had to use some creative wording to ask around so it wouldn't seem suspicious. I'd worked with another agent, Brandon Hayes, last year so got in touch with him. I told him I had a CI who had brought up Mike Nicholson in an interrogation and we wanted to make sure what he'd told us was true. We said the CI told us he'd been roughed up by him and asked if that's the kind of agent he is. Brandon was emphatic that the CI must be lying because Nicholson goes by the book. There was no way he would have used physical force unless he was defending himself, of course. I don't have any reason to believe he would lie to us which makes me think Nicholson can be trusted and it had to be someone else who leaked the information about Lily's evidence."

"Or he's been very good at covering himself," Sarah suggested.

"It's a possibility, but I'm inclined to disregard that angle," Phil replied. His scowl had disappeared and his tone had lost the edge of anger from earlier.

"In that case, we'll trust your judgement," Vivian said.

"So, what should we do next?" Meghan asked, and then regretted it as soon as the words were out of her mouth when Phil turned his death stare on her.

"*You* shouldn't do anything," he snarled.

Chapter 28

The sky was dotted with puffy white clouds breaking up the expanse of brilliant blue and adding texture to the sky. Had it not been for the warmth of the sun, the day would have been cold rather than the typical crisp chill of autumn for this time of year. A flock of geese flew overhead honking as they passed the somber group below. They were huddled around a gravesite and a marker engraved with Lily's name and the dates of her birth and death. She would be resting beside the graves of her parents. The only attendees were a priest, Meghan, Vivian, and the four members of the Cozy Quilts Club. That's how Vivian wanted it and how she imagined Lily would have wanted it. After the priest had recited the passages Vivian had chosen for the service and took his leave, Sarah laid a spray of flowers from the Club on top of Lily's casket beside the ones Vivian and Meghan had already placed there. Meghan wiped her eyes and handed another tissue from her purse to Vivian.

Annalise felt the hairs on the back of her neck rising and leaned over to Jennifer standing beside her. "Take your phone out and pretend you're reading a text. We're going to turn around to leave and I want you to be ready to take a picture of the man standing behind us to our right. It's okay to look up but try to avoid looking directly at him. You need to make it seem like you're looking at your screen so he won't realize you're taking his photo."

Jennifer knew Annalise hadn't turned around to actually see who was standing there, but she also knew that she must have had a vision of the man she was referring to. She nodded her head slightly to acknowledge she had heard Annalise and reached into her purse for her phone as she'd been instructed.

Annalise then quietly spoke to the others to let them know what was happening and cautioned them as well not to pay attention to the man. "Give Jennifer and me a head start before you leave. It might spook him if we all turn around at once." The air became charged as they all nodded that they understood.

"I just got a text from David. I'm going to need to leave now," Jennifer told the group, holding up her phone and speaking louder than she usually would. She had no idea if the man was close enough to hear, but thought it would add a convincing touch, just in case. She faked typing a message on her phone, and they turned to leave. She held up her phone again, pretending to be reading. She had the camera app already queued up and when the image of a man standing beside a car parked to their right appeared on the screen, pushed the button several times to take his photo. The photo wasn't centered because of the angle where he was standing away from her, but she thought she caught enough of his features to identify him later.

"Do you think you got him?" Annalise spoke softly, her head bowed.

"I did. They won't be getting any awards for best photography, but there should be more detail when we enlarge them so Dennis and Phil will have enough to go on."

As soon as the man spotted Annalise and Jennifer walking toward their car parked in the dirt lane running between the grave plots, he quickly walked away from the gravesite he was pretending to study and drove slowly away.

"How did he even know we were here?" Jennifer asked.

"That's a very good question."

Chapter 29

Annalise and Jennifer drove to Meghan's apartment where they had all agreed to meet following the graveside service. Eva, Sarah, and Ashley arrived in Eva's car followed by Meghan and Vivian minutes later. Once settled into Meghan's apartment, Jennifer showed them the pictures.

As soon as she saw the Patriots cap, Eva's eyes lit up. "That's what Panda was trying to describe when he told me about the insignia on the baseball hat!"

"That's the guy who was at our house," Sarah said.

"He's the man who was at the storage unit, too," Annalise said.

"Why would he be at the cemetery?" Vivian wondered aloud.

"More to the point, how did he find out *we* would be there then? You didn't post an obituary, did you?" she asked Vivian.

"No, I didn't. Other than all of you, the only ones who knew were the people at the funeral home."

"They couldn't possibly be connected to the drug ring, could they?" Meghan asked incredulously.

"There's got to be another explanation," Eva said. "That funeral home is an institution in the Bangor area. I can't believe they'd risk their reputation or even need to be involved with anything illegal."

"If the drug ring has a mole inside the police, they could have found out where Lily's body was being taken when the coroner released it," Sarah suggested, her brow furrowed in thought. "I suppose they could have made up some story about why they needed to know when her service was going to be held…"

"That makes the most sense," Annalise agreed. "I think we should share this with Dennis and Phil sooner than later. If they've got a mole working in their department, they need to find out who it is, and this is more widespread than one dirty cop."

Jennifer scrolled to her Contacts and hit Call.

"Dennis, it's Jennifer Ryder. We have more information for you, and we need to talk ASAP."

Chapter 30

"I took these pictures at the cemetery during Lily's graveside service," Jennifer explained as she handed her phone over to the detectives.

Phil scrolled through the pictures as Dennis looked on but neither of them showed any sign of recognition of the man in the photos.

"I don't recognize him," Phil said, looking at Dennis to see if he did.

"Neither do I. Would you email these to me? I can check with a guy I know who I can ask without arousing any suspicions."

"Maybe you have some ideas about how he would have found out about the service? There was no obituary published with the information and other than us, only the funeral home knew," Vivian asked.

The detectives came to the same conclusion that Sarah had.

"At some point, we'll have to get Internal Affairs involved if the leak is with us," Phil said, addressing Dennis.

"I agree, but we don't have enough to go on yet. Not to mention that this isn't even our case."

"Unless there's anything else you have to tell us, we'll say goodnight," Phil said after a pause in which everyone was silent.

"That's all we had for now," Sarah said, looking to the others who shook their heads indicating they had nothing new to share.

"Is anyone else feeling as discouraged as I am?" Meghan asked. The glum expression on her face was mirrored on the faces of everyone else in the room, making the question moot.

"Don't give up, Meghan. We've had this happen to us with our other cases but in the end, we were able to discover who the killer was, and they were arrested. It seems hopeless right now, but my intuition is telling me not to give up. Something will come our way to bring us closer to solving this mystery, too," Annalise said.

"I wish I didn't have to go home tomorrow so I could help, but my bereavement leave is up, and I have to go back to my job," Vivian said apologetically.

"We understand. There's not much more we can do until the DEA agent gets back from vacation," Meghan reassured her.

"Now, see? We *do* have something more coming our way!" Annalise's enthusiasm was contagious and the mood in the room shifted from glum to optimistic.

Chapter 31

Meghan's brows furrowed when the name **Detective Brooks** displayed on her phone's screen. *What does he want?* She forced herself to keep the annoyance she felt out of her voice when she answered the call.

"Ms. Doherty, I need you to come to the station to discuss new information we received regarding your whereabouts at the time Ms. Sullivan was killed."

Meghan didn't respond immediately as her mind was trying to make sense of what Detective Brooks was saying. She could feel her heartbeat speeding up along with her anxiety.

"Ms. Doherty?"

"Yes, I'm here. Isn't this something you can discuss over the phone.? I'm at work now and can't take time off."

"No, we need to have this on record. What time do you take your lunch break? We can do it then."

He's not going to give me any other option. "Fine. I can be there at one, but I have to be back at my office by two, so we'll have to make it quick."

Meghan arrived promptly at one and was greeted by Brooks who was waiting in the reception area. He ushered them back to the same conference room they'd been in during her first one-on-one meeting with him. She fought the urge to shift in her seat, her nervousness threatening to take hold. *Don't fidget! It makes you look guilty* she cautioned herself. His surly attitude had not improved since the last time they'd met. If anything, she sensed even more hostility emanating from him as he turned on the digital recorder, then announced their names and the time and date.

"I received a call from Brian Jackson. He said he lives in the apartment next to yours. According to him, you were with him when Ms. Sullivan was killed. He said you told him you were going to check on your cat. That would have been shortly before you found her. Why didn't you tell me this earlier? And why did you make up the story about going for a walk?"

Meghan was stunned. "Because it's not true."

"The walk or being with Brian Jackson?"

"I wasn't with Brian. I had taken a walk, just like I told you." Meghan's voice was getting louder, and her words were clipped.

"Did you convince him to make it up to give yourself an alibi?"

"Of course not!"

"Why would he lie about it?"

"I have no idea. It's no secret that Brian has a crush on me, but I'm not interested in him in that way. Maybe he thought he was doing me a favor. How do I know? I haven't even talked to him since a couple days after Lily was murdered. And besides, wouldn't it make me look even more like I was lying about taking a walk if all of a sudden, I talked Brian into telling you I was with him?"

Brooks was silent and repeated the staring contest tactic just as he had during their first interview, but Meghan didn't take the bait this time either. He finally gave up and turned off the recorder after stating the interview was completed. He walked to the door and opened it, signaling that Meghan was free to leave and led her back to the reception area.

"You might want to have a word with Mr. Jackson. I won't press charges this time for filing a false report but there won't be a second chance."

He didn't bother waiting for her response before turning around and walking back to his office.

"You can bet I will," she muttered.

⸺

"WHAT WERE YOU THINKING, Brian? Detective Brooks already has his sights set on me for killing Lily. He accused me of trying to have you give me an alibi by making up that story I was with you."

Meghan was standing in the hallway with her hands on her hips. She hadn't even entered Brian's apartment after he opened the door to let loose on him. She'd been fuming about this all afternoon.

"I'm sorry. I'm sorry. I heard you didn't have an alibi so I thought I could help. I didn't think it through. Don't be mad at me," Brian's voice had taken on a whining tone and he was wringing his hands.

The door of the apartment next to them opened and Barry Hopkins popped his head outside.

"Everything okay there?" he asked.

Nice job, Meghan. Now all the neighbors on the floor know you're a murder suspect. "Sorry, Mr. Hopkins. We're fine," Meghan replied, pasting on a smile.

He gave each of them an appraising look, grunted and shut his door. Brian moved aside and she walked into his apartment away from prying eyes.

Meghan's anger turned to pity for Brian as he stood there with a contrite expression.

She sighed and all the pent-up frustration she'd felt the last several hours deflated.

"You could have been arrested for filing a false police report. Detective Brooks told me he wouldn't do that, but warned me that he wouldn't give you another chance."

"I was just trying to help."

"I get that, Brian, but it complicated things instead. It made me look like I was lying about being out of the apartment and taking the walk when Lily was killed."

"I'd heard you and Lily arguing and…"

"*Wait.* Do you think I was the one who killed her?" Meghan asked incredulously.

Brian stepped back, realizing he'd made a mistake.

"No, no, of course not. I mean, not intentionally. I thought maybe it was an accident. You were fighting and then it got quiet, so I turned the volume on my TV back down, but a little later, it sounded like you were fighting again. When I heard that Lily died from a head wound, I thought you might have pushed each other, and she fell and hit her head," he finished lamely.

Meghan stood staring at him with her mouth open.

"Wow! I can't believe you said that… or that you would even think that I could have done that. Or, worse, that I would have waited an hour before calling anyone and tried to convince the police someone else had come into our apartment while I was out."

Brian knew he'd put his foot in his mouth and made a huge mistake. His face contorted and Meghan saw what was coming.

"Don't you dare start crying!"

He started to speak, but Meghan held up her hand to stop him.

"I think it's better if you don't say anything else. I'm too angry right now and should leave before I say something I'll regret." She was about to leave but stopped to add one more thought. "By the way, that's why I left the day Lily and I fought. I didn't want to lose our friendship because I was angry, and I would *never* have put my hands on her or hurt her. I thought you knew me better."

She closed his door softly behind her. She was still angry, but it was mixed with sadness that Brian had even considered she was capable of killing Lily, whether intentionally or by accident.

Chapter 32

A week went by without any breaks in the case and the frustration for the team was beginning to show. The detectives had reached out to their lead with Jennifer's photos, but it had been a dead end. Their only hope was that the DEA Agent would have success where they had failed.

Meghan was lying down on her couch and Panda was curled up beside her tucked in between her body and the back cushion. The warmth of Panda's body against her leg gave her a sense of comfort. The apartment had felt lonely since Vivian had returned to Massachusetts. It was the first time Meghan had spent more than a day in it alone since she and Lily had moved in together. The TV was on, but it was more for background noise than entertainment. She found it difficult to concentrate and her thoughts kept drifting. Her phone rang, making her jump, which in turn woke Panda, who leaped off the couch but instead of running into the bedroom, he stretched in a perfect cat yoga posture as if to say he meant to do that all along.

"I heard from Agent Nicholson!" Vivian exclaimed before Meghan even had a chance to say hello.

"You did? When?" Meghan sat straight up when she heard the news.

"I just got off the phone with him. I've been checking my phone every day and turning it off to make sure it's not tapped. I'd written down his number from Lily's journal so told him I'd call him back. It could have been anyone impersonating him, so I thought that was the best way to make sure he was legit."

"That was smart," Meghan said.

"He's back from vacation and found out today about Lily. She had given him my name and number to contact in case anything happened to her. He knew she'd kept her own recordings and journal, but he hasn't seen or heard them, and he wants to do that tomorrow. I told him I couldn't be there, but he should get in touch with you and Sarah."

"Did you tell him the rest of what's happened and what we found out?"

"Not in a lot of detail and suggested he should get in touch with you to find out the rest. Besides, Sarah's the one who can give him access to the copies. I told him I wanted your permission first, though, before I gave him your number. Is that okay?"

"Of course! Maybe now we can wrap this case up."

Meghan's phone rang again five minutes later. The screen display read Unknown Caller but she answered thinking it must be Agent Nicholson. The voice on the other end was a deep baritone.

"Ms. Doherty?"

"Yes, that's me."

"Vivian Sullivan suggested I call you regarding her sister, Lily."

"Yes, she let me know I should expect your call. She also mentioned you would like more information about the envelope Lily left for Vivian, and I should meet with you to discuss that. Would you be able to meet me tomorrow at The Sandwich Shop on Central Street? I'd need to do this on my lunch break which is from one to two. Does that work for you?"

"I can make that work. How will I recognize you?"

Meghan almost giggled as a visual image popped into her head of a red rose pinned to a jacket lapel that she'd seen in a number of movies. Instead, she described the coat she would be wearing. Almost as if on cue, when she asked how she would recognize him, he told her not to worry, he'd find her.

Her next call was to Sarah.

"Meet me at The Sandwich Shop at one tomorrow. I think we've caught a break!"

Chapter 33

Meghan took her lunch break a few minutes early so she could be at The Sandwich Shop before one. The lunch crowd was shifting as the noon to one break diners left and the one to two crowd was beginning to arrive. It was a popular spot for downtown workers, and she realized it might not be the best choice if they weren't able to find a table. There were two people in front of her placing their orders at the front counter but as she waited, she scanned the table seating area to her left. She'd never counted the number of tables there before, but she guessed there might be at least a dozen and at two of them, the diners were picking up their trays preparing to leave. She sent a silent prayer that the customers placing their orders ahead of her would be take-out orders. She jumped when she felt a tap on her shoulder and then relaxed when she recognized Sarah's voice.

"Sorry, didn't mean to scare you."

"No problem. Guess I'm nervous about meeting…" she hesitated debating whether to say his name out loud. "… our guest," she landed on. "Tell me what you want, and I'll put in the order so you can grab that table in the far corner where those people are leaving."

She moved to the head of the line and was about to give her order to the woman behind the counter when she heard the baritone voice from the night before and a tall, well-built man in his thirties stood beside her. He was dressed casually in jeans and a lightweight jacket that was unzipped and exposed the blue button-down shirt he wore underneath it. He had dark brown hair and brown eyes in a face so handsome, Meghan almost forgot to breathe.

"I'll get this," he told the clerk and turned to Meghan. "What would you like, Meghan?"

She could only stare for several seconds before she came back to reality as he waited patiently.

"Oh, right. I was going to give them Sarah's order, too, if that's okay?" When he raised his eyebrows, she realized she hadn't told him about Sarah the night before. "She's a friend of mine and Lily's," she explained. "She's at the table over in the corner." She turned to Sarah who waved at them, aware of what must be going on between Meghan and her companion. He looked to the table where Sarah was seated and nodded his understanding. The clerk had been tapping her finger on the cash register, not bothering to hide her annoyance at the amount of time it was taking them. Meghan gave their selections to the clerk and waited while he added his choice to the order. Once the bill was paid, they were handed a plastic numbered sign mounted in a short metal frame to identify their order to the server who would bring it to their table.

Meghan sat beside Sarah and Agent Nicholson took the seat opposite which faced the entrance.

"Sarah, this is…"

"Just call me Mike," he interrupted, extending his hand for Sarah to shake. "Meghan tells me you're a friend of Lily's?"

"That's right. But before we go any further, I'd like to see some ID."

Agent Nicholson's eyebrows raised but he took out his

wallet and produced his ID and driver's license for Sarah's inspection.

"Okay. I have information that might be able to help you that I've stored in a secure location. Vivian shared it with me because at my day job, I'm a cybersecurity technician. Lily left instructions that Vivian should pass the information on to you if anything happened to her. So that's why we're here."

"Do you have it with you?"

"No, you'll have to come with me to my house where I can access the files," she said and then addressed Meghan, "Did you tell Mike about what's happened since Lily died?"

"Not yet, but this may be too public a place to do that."

The hard surfaces created acoustics in the shop that made conversation difficult unless you spoke louder than normal. Once again, Meghan realized her choice of this location, although convenient to where she worked, wasn't the best for their exchange of information.

"Could I follow you to your house when we leave, and you can bring me up to speed there at the same time as you're sharing the rest of the information Lily had for me?"

Sarah quickly ran through her workload for the rest of the day before agreeing to his plan.

"I'm sorry to rush this along since you haven't had a chance to finish your lunch, but I'd like to get to this now," Mike said.

Meghan and Sarah were initially put off by his brusqueness but could see the logic of his suggestion since they weren't able to tell him all that he needed to know in the sandwich shop. There was a supply of cardboard boxes on the table with napkins and cutlery for customers to make their own to-go containers. Meghan brought three back to the table and they wrapped the rest of their lunches inside to eat later. Sarah gave Mike her address and twenty minutes later, they were ensconced in Sarah's home office. Max was keeping watch from his bed in front of the window.

Mike listened as Sarah told him about the theft of the envelope, the apartment being bugged, and the trip to the storage unit.

"Shoot, I just remembered I didn't get copies of the photos Jennifer took of the guy who showed up at my house and then at the cemetery. I'm going to text her now and ask her to send them to me."

The ping on her computer alerted them they'd arrived in her email inbox, and she downloaded them to her desktop.

"That's Randy Hughes. He was Lily's dealer," Mike said when he'd examined the photos. "You said he showed up at your house and the cemetery?"

Sarah gave him the details of both occasions.

"What we haven't been able to figure out is how did he and his boss find out that Lily was keeping the journal and recordings if only she and you knew about them and how did they know we'd be at the cemetery? And why did he come to my house? It makes sense that they could have figured out I was involved from listening in when the apartment was bugged and Meghan suggested bringing them to me. But the cemetery…?" She let the question hang in the air.

"I don't have an explanation. At least, not yet, but I have some ideas about where to look for answers," Mike said. "In the meantime, can you bring up the journal and recordings so I can take a look?"

They spent the next hour going through Lily's information and Sarah made a copy on a USB drive for Mike to take with him. But only after he convinced her it would be safe with him despite the possibility of the leak being in his department.

"Will you keep us in the loop?" she asked.

"As much as I can."

"That's not especially convincing," Sarah said.

"Best I can do."

Chapter 34

"How did it go?" Meghan asked, her voice eager.

Instead of calling, Meghan had shown up at Sarah's house, unable to wait for Sarah to call to tell her what had happened during her meeting with Mike. They were seated at the table in Sarah's kitchen along with Ashley. Meghan's stomach growled as the aroma of the beef stew in the crockpot and a fresh loaf of homemade bread filled the room. She'd never had the chance to finish the half-eaten sandwich she packed earlier in the to-go box, and it was still in the break room's refrigerator. In her eagerness to see Sarah, she'd completely forgotten to take it with her at the end of her workday.

"I couldn't really get a read on him. He was surprised by some of the entries in Lily's journal and her recordings that took place after he'd gone on vacation. I questioned him about how anyone could have known about that and the rest of the times Randy Hughes… Yes, he confirmed that's who it was when he saw the pictures," Sarah said anticipating Meghan's question. "But how he could have known where I lived or when we'd be at the cemetery?"

"Is he going to check?" Meghan asked, her frustration matching what Sarah had felt earlier.

"He said he would, as much as he can, but that was '*the best he could do*'." The use of air quotes and the sarcasm in her voice told Meghan all she needed to know about Sarah's opinion of Mike Nicholson..

Meghan's shoulders sagged as her earlier excitement retreated. It seemed there was no end to the lack of progress and every new clue led to yet another roadblock.

"Do you think we can trust him?"

Sarah considered the question thinking back to her afternoon with Mike and her impressions of him. Whether she trusted him wasn't the same as what she thought of his professionalism. She also didn't want to add to Meghan's disappointment. She'd noticed how haggard Meghan looked lately and realized how much it must be weighing on her that she was still the primary suspect in Detective Brooks's opinion. That wouldn't change until the case was solved and the true killer was in custody.

"I didn't have the sense that he is involved in any sort of cover up," she said, carefully weighing her words. "I suppose I should give him the benefit of the doubt since I really don't know him or his work ethics. And from what Phil and Dennis told us, we can trust him. It could be that he's someone who keeps things close to the vest and didn't want to reveal more of what he knows to me. He doesn't know us either or whether he can trust us. It's possible he got enough from what Lily left for him to move things forward but didn't want to say so."

Meghan's face brightened and she felt a spark of optimism return.

"That's true. I shouldn't be giving up so easily."

Sarah said a silent prayer that she hadn't given Meghan false hope.

"Would you like to stay for dinner? We have plenty,"

Ashley offered, reading Sarah's mood, and sensing it was time to change the subject.

"Have you heard my stomach growling?" Meghan asked, her cheeks turning a faint shade of pink.

"Just a little," Ashley replied, giving Meghan a smile.

⊏⊐

DINNER HAD BEEN DELICIOUS, and it felt good to be with other people. Panda helped keep her company, but it wasn't the same. Meghan was reluctant to return to her empty apartment but didn't want to overstay her welcome. Panda came running as soon as she opened the door; whether that was because his dish was empty or he was happy to see her, Meghan couldn't say and didn't want to dwell on the answer. The quiet in the apartment was oppressive and the first thing Meghan did after feeding Panda was to turn on the television. Anything to distract her from the silence. She sat on the couch, tucking her feet up and reached for the throw that was draped over the back cushions. It had been Lily's first project when she learned how to knit and was made of a soft bulky yarn in shades of black and white. Lily had been so proud of that blanket. Meghan pulled it up under her arms and tucked it in around her legs. She channel surfed with the remote before landing on a home improvement show but her gaze wandered to the photos of herself and Lily scattered around the room. Her gaze landed on a selfie photo of them during their sorority days.

"We had some good times then, didn't we?"

A smile curved her lips as she thought back to the day that picture had been taken. They had moved from their dorms into the sorority house as new pledges and were assigned as roommates. Over the next three years the bond they formed continued to grow. As graduation day loomed closer, they knew they still wanted to be roommates and had moved into this apartment.

Seeing Lily's face smiling back at her, Meghan burst into tears.

"I'm sorry, Lily. We're really trying to catch the man who killed you."

The tears kept coming until she'd finally cried herself out and Panda jumped up in her lap and butted his head against her face, his purrs vibrating against her chest. She snuggled her face against his neck and rubbed his back, soaking in all the comfort he gave. Their tender moment was interrupted by a loud knocking at the door.

"Who can that be at this time of night?" Panda didn't answer. He jumped down and ran to the bedrooms before she even had a chance to finish the question. Her surprise turned to concern, wondering who would be knocking on her door this late at night. Her chest tightened when she peeked through the peephole in the door and spied Detective Brooks standing there, a sour expression on his face. *Now what?* Whatever it was, she knew it couldn't be good, but she had no choice but to open the door.

"Meghan Doherty, you're under arrest."

Chapter 35

This can't be happening. This can't be happening. The words drummed in her head on a loop.

She had been read her Miranda rights and was told she had been arrested for possession with intent to sell illegal drugs. Her car had been searched and a bag of oxycontin was found hidden in her trunk under the compartment for the tire jack. She felt numb and barely present as she was taken to booking, processed, fingerprinted, and a mug shot taken. Now she was in an interrogation room with Detective Brooks, wearing a smug look on his face.

"How long had you been dealing drugs with Lily Sullivan?"

"What? I *wasn't* dealing drugs with Lily… or anyone, for that matter."

"Then perhaps you can explain the drugs we found in your car?" he pressed on.

"I can't explain it. I suppose Lily could have put them in there at some point. Or someone is trying to frame me," she said, her face defiant as that explanation occurred to her. Considering what had happened since Lily's death, it wasn't outside the realm of possibility.

"That's very convenient; blaming it on someone who can't defend themselves."

"That's not what I'm saying," Meghan objected. "It would explain how you got a warrant to search my car, though. How else would you think to do that if someone hadn't tipped you off?"

"We got the warrant legally. That's really all you need to know."

He opened the file he'd brought in with him, and had placed on the table unopened. He began flipping through the pages and not so subtly arranging one of the crime scene photos so that it was partially exposed for Meghan to see underneath the other papers on top.

"So, here's the way I see it," Brooks resumed his interrogation. "You and Lily Sullivan were in this together. She wanted out but you didn't. The two of you argued about it. It got physical and you pushed her. She hit her head on the counter. When you checked for a pulse, she was dead. Instead of calling 911, you panicked and decided to go for a walk to get out of the apartment and come up with a plan claiming you found her that way when you got back."

"*No*, I already told you, when I left, she was still alive…"

"Yeah, that's what you told me," Brooks said, sarcastically.

There's no point even trying to defend myself. He's already made up his mind, she thought, and remained silent as they sat staring at each other, waiting for one of them to flinch.

His face softened when he realized she wasn't going to break, playing the roles of good cop, bad cop on his own.

"Look, it was an accident, right? You never meant to kill her. Just admit it and we can probably get the charges reduced from homicide to involuntary manslaughter," he said.

"I told you I didn't do it. You obviously don't believe me, so now I want a lawyer."

Bad cop quickly returned, and his face darkened, realizing

his questioning was done now that she'd requested a lawyer. He gave her a disgusted look, picked up the file and stormed out of the room.

Chapter 36

"You're *where?*" Sarah asked, not believing she'd heard right.

"I'm in the county jail. They arrested me last night."

"Why didn't you call me then? I could have come right away so you wouldn't have to stay there all night."

"It was really late by the time they got through booking me and I didn't want to bother you. It wasn't that bad."

"Did Brooks finally arrest you for killing Lily?"

"No. They found drugs hidden in the trunk of my car and arrested me for possession with intent to sell, and Brooks is trying to scare me into confessing to killing Lily. I finally asked for a lawyer, so he had to stop. They've appointed me a public defender since I don't have a lawyer I can call. I hate to ask you this, but could you post bail for me?"

"Of course. Well, I think I can. How much will it be?" Sarah asked.

Meghan gave her the details, and Sarah was relieved to hear it was an amount she would be able to cover.

"What's going on?" Ashley asked when Sarah was off the phone. There hadn't been enough information from the half of the conversation she'd heard to grasp the full gist of what was happening.

"Meghan's been arrested on a drug charge. It's a set up and my bet is on Randy Hughes being the one who orchestrated it along with his police buddy. Would it be alright with you if I bring her back here? I'm worried about her being safe alone in her apartment," Sarah said. "We'll probably have to bring Panda with us," she added as an afterthought.

"Of course! Do you know how Panda is around dogs?"

"I guess we'll find out," Sarah said, smiling.

Chapter 37

Sarah returned two hours later with Meghan in tow, carrying an overnight bag, cat care, food and equipment, and a cat carrier with a very unhappy Panda inside. Max managed to extricate himself from Ashley's grip and bounded forward to greet them. As soon as he started sniffing the cat carrier, Panda gave out a loud hiss and backed himself into the far corner of the cage. Max backed up and looked at Sarah for reassurance.

"It's okay, Max. Panda is going to be staying with us for a while so you'll need to give him some space to adjust."

"I'm sorry, he's not used to dogs. I'll take him upstairs and put him in the guest room along with my things," Meghan said, apologetically.

"No worries. We'll figure it out," Ashley said, giving her a hug.

"How's she doing?" Ashley asked Sarah when Meghan was out of earshot. They had taken the cat food and supplies into the kitchen until they could figure out the best place to put them that would make them accessible to Panda but out of Max's reach.

"She's putting on a brave face, but I can tell that underneath the bravado she's worried. Actually, that might be an understatement. I think she's terrified," Sarah replied. "They couldn't arrest her for Lily's death, but they have the drugs they found in her trunk as evidence. She has an appointment with her attorney this afternoon and asked me to go with her. We're going to tell her what we have found out so far, including what was in Lily's envelope and what they found in the storage locker. It will be protected by the attorney-client privilege, and we agreed her attorney should know everything so that she'll be in a better position to defend Meghan."

"I need to get some work done, so I'll see you two at lunchtime," Ashley said, nodding slightly to alert Sarah, whose back was turned so she couldn't see that Meghan was approaching. "Try not to worry. You're not alone in this," she told Meghan, gently squeezing her arm before going to her office upstairs.

"I should get some work done, too," Sarah said after she and Meghan decided the best place to put the cat food, water, and litter box would be the guest bathroom, at least until Panda felt safer. "Will you be okay by yourself for a few hours?"

"Sure. Knowing you and Ashley are here with me makes me feel a lot better. I should probably write down what I want to say when we meet with the attorney so I don't get anxious and forget things. I can't thank you enough for all you've done for me." Meghan's eyes were glistening, but she kept the tears from flowing.

"That's what friends are for, right?" Sarah said, keeping her tone light.

Meghan nodded, too emotional to respond. Following her upstairs, they parted ways when Sarah turned into her office and Meghan continued down the hallway to the guest room. She opened the door carefully so Panda wouldn't escape but found him, growling softly, still huddled in his carrier even though its door was unlatched. She knelt down so she could look inside and met his eyes, hoping he would be encouraged to come out as she spoke to him in a hushed voice. Her efforts were in vain, though.

"I get it, buddy. You're upset with me for taking you out of our house and bringing you here. As if that wasn't bad enough, there's a dog. You take your time. I'm not going to force you to come out."

Better just make the best of it she thought, resigning herself to being here for... *however long it takes, I guess.* She opened her overnight bag and removed its contents to place them in the drawers of the bureau tucked against the wall perpendicular to the bed. That done, she took out her laptop and began documenting all that had happened since the day she'd found Lily in their kitchen.

Chapter 38

"I think he must have come out while Sarah and I were at the attorney's office," Meghan was telling Ashley in response to her question about how Panda was doing. Ashley had found a gate they had used to block off parts of the house when Max was a puppy and still not housebroken. They'd placed it in the hallway so that the guest bedroom and bathroom were inaccessible to Max until Panda was more acclimated. Meghan had put his food, water, and litter box in the bathroom, which was not ideal, but it would have to do.

They were gathered at the kitchen table enjoying their dinner and glasses of wine. Meghan was in a more positive mood after the appointment with her attorney.

"Are you feeling confident she'll do a good job?" Ashley asked.

"I'm cautiously optimistic but that's not a reflection on her. She warned me that the best she could do was give me the best defense possible, but it would be up to a jury to decide."

"What did she think about all that's happened with the connection to Lily? I'm guessing she thought this was just a drug charge before your appointment."

"That's right. We really didn't get into it when we set up

the appointment after she was assigned my case. When she heard all the rest of it, her attitude did a one-eighty. She's had cases where Brooks was involved before, and she has the same opinion of him as Phil and Dennis do."

"She was a little concerned about their involvement since they're not assigned to the case but I think we reassured her that they wouldn't do anything to jeopardize it," Sarah interjected.

"What about Agent Nicholson? Is she going to get in touch with him?" Ashley asked.

"She wasn't sure if she would contact him directly yet. We told her what Phil and Dennis found out about him, but she still wanted to wait until she was able to ask her own contacts at the DEA if he's trustworthy," Meghan said. "Either way, though, she wants to know what they're doing about the drug situation. Her feeling is that if there's an ongoing case involving the dealer, it's all going to be tied in together and that will affect my case."

"Especially since it's obvious it was a set-up and circumstantial," Sarah added.

"Even though the drugs were found in Meghan's car?" Ashley asked.

"That complicates things and is one of the things she was cautioning us about since it could rest in the hands of a jury if the charges aren't dismissed before it gets that far," Meghan said.

The conversation stalled as they each contemplated the stakes of solving the case.

Chapter 39

Ashley and Meghan were in the living room watching television when Sarah burst into the room. They looked up, startled by her abrupt entrance and the look of excitement on her face. Max, who had been asleep on the floor, jumped up and let out a *woof!* before he realized it was Sarah, not a stranger in the room. Looking sheepish, he lowered his head, tail wagging as he went over to Sarah and licked her hand.

"It's okay, buddy. Sorry I scared you." She stroked his head to reassure him that she wasn't upset with him.

"You've got to come see this!" she said, gesturing for them to follow her upstairs. When they entered her office, there was a video paused on her computer monitor. She took her seat and clicked the mouse to start it playing.

"That's me!" Meghan exclaimed. "That's from the day Lily was killed and I walked down to the waterfront. Where did you find that?"

"I may have hacked into a couple of security cameras, but you didn't hear that from me," Sarah grinned. "And look at the date and time stamp. It proves you were there exactly like you said you were."

Meghan's eyes lit up when the solid proof for her alibi was verified on the videotape.

"But wait, there's more," Sarah grinned, and began fast rewinding the video. She stopped when she reached the time stamp she had written on a piece of scratch paper. Both Meghan and Ashley sucked in their breath when they saw the scene playing out before them.

Chapter 40

"We have to show this to my attorney... and Phil and Dennis," Meghan said when Sarah stopped the video.

"And Agent Nicholson?" Ashley said, more as a question than a statement.

"I agree," Sarah said. "It's too late to do that tonight, but first thing tomorrow we should call them and have them meet us here tomorrow night after you are back from work."

The day seemed to stretch on forever for all of them, but finally at the appointed time Phil, Dennis and Mike arrived and Sarah led them to her office where she replayed both sections of the video just as she had the night before for Meghan and Ashley. Sarah had explained why they would all be there when she'd asked them to come.

"That's Lily and Randy Hughes!" Agent Nicholson said when Sarah queued that section up. "But who's the other guy?" he said, more to himself than the others in the room. The man in the video had his back to the camera and never turned his head so they could see his face. When they'd entered the frame, Randy Hughes was obstructing any clear view of his face.

"There's something familiar about him, but I can't put my

finger on it," Dennis said, shaking his head in response to Mike's question.

"Same here," Phil added.

"How did you get this?" Mike asked.

"Might be better not to ask, but if say, hypothetically, of course, you were to check the security camera footage for the Waterfront Restaurant Bar & Grille, you might find this. I might have, again hypothetically, made a copy of it just in case they tape over their video footage but it's probably better to request it through proper channels ASAP from them. I was only looking for evidence that Meghan had been at the water- front like she said she was but when I was rewinding the video, I went too far and couldn't believe it when I recognized Lily and saw she was there earlier that day. I don't know if she'll be able to use it in court, but I'm planning to make a copy for Meghan's attorney, too, as insurance in case Brooks tries to arrest Meghan for Lily's murder along with the drug charge."

The men all nodded their understanding.

"Would you run it again, please?" Mike asked, and Sarah obliged. "Stop it there! Can you zoom in on their hands?"

"It looks like she's handing him money," Sarah said.

"And it's the other guy, not Randy, who's taking it," Mike added.

"Which means… ?" Sarah asked.

"We can connect him to associating with Randy Hughes, a known drug dealer. The only reason Lily was with Randy was to do a drug deal. And if we can match any of her recordings to that same day and time, it would be even better."

Chapter 41

"Have you figured out how Randy Hughes and the other guy knew Lily was working as a CI for you?" Sarah asked. They had all gathered in the living room after Sarah's demonstration.

"Not exactly. There are signs that someone hacked into my computer and got into my files while I was on vacation even though they were password protected, but I haven't been able to nail down who did it. Hughes and his boss must have begun to suspect she was working for me. We'd been as careful as we could about how we contacted each other, but we must have been at the wrong place at the wrong time, and someone saw us who shouldn't have."

"That makes sense. It's more likely the leak is in the DEA than with us," Phil said.

Nicholson bristled but Dennis stepped in to diffuse the situation.

"We know there's a dirty cop in our department. We're not trying to deny that, but in our defense, we didn't have any reason at that point to suspect Lily was involved with drugs. She'd never been arrested and by all accounts was a model citizen. She wasn't on our radar. Doesn't it seem more reasonable that Hughes and his boss would have suspected the DEA was involved since they're dealing drugs?"

Nicholson considered that and finally nodded his head. "I see your point."

"We can try to dig into things from our side, but we have to be careful we don't give anything away. It's not our case, but because of this lady and her friends, we're willing to help," Dennis said, looking at Sarah.

"If it wasn't for their help, three killers might have gone free," Phil agreed.

"How?" Nicholson asked.

"That's between us," Dennis said. "You'll just have to take our word for it."

"Okay," Nicholson decided there was no point trying to push it.

"They've made more progress on this case than Brooks ever would. It's too bad we can't use it, though," Dennis said.

"Do you know who tipped them off about the drugs in my car?" Meghan asked.

"No. The tip was anonymous and there was no way to trace it, but my money is on Randy Hughes. He and his boss want you behind bars for this so the case will be closed," Phil said.

"Isn't there anyone who could work with you behind the scenes?" Sarah asked.

"I've been thinking about that very thing, and I might have someone," Nicholson said.

Chapter 42

Everyone's attention was focused on Mike and there was an undercurrent of excitement in the room.

"There's a prosecutor I've worked with before and she's tough on drug dealers. Especially those higher on the food chain. She's also someone I trust implicitly to keep this under wraps until we're ready to make any arrests."

"What's her name?" Phil interrupted.

"It's Danielle Larson," Mike said. "I was planning to take my evidence to her once I found out who Randy's boss was."

"I've never worked with her directly, but she's got a good reputation with cops. She's got a high conviction rate, but not because she cuts corners. She's thorough with her preparation for trial and expects the evidence we provide to be top notch. She wouldn't put up with someone like Brooks," Phil continued.

"Do you think she'd be okay with us working with you on this?" Dennis asked.

Mike thought for a moment before replying. "I think it's best that I approach her first and tell her how you're involved, and we can go from there."

"Okay, sounds fair," Phil agreed.

"Do I have to wait to show my attorney the videos?" Meghan asked.

The three cops looked to each other in silence for their decision. Mike was the first one to offer an opinion. He shrugged his shoulders and then turned to Meghan. "If you can wait until I've spoken to Danielle, I'd appreciate it. She may want to bring her in anyway. You said she's a public defender?"

"I hadn't, but, yes, she is," Meghan said, her cheeks flushing with embarrassment. She felt it reflected poorly on her that she wasn't able to afford a private attorney.

"That could be a problem. Even though she's under the same umbrella, she's on the opposite side. It might be a conflict of interest," Mike said, and sighed and then brightened. "You could show her just the portion of the video that proves your alibi. It doesn't have anything directly to do with the drug deal with Lily. Sarah, you can edit that part out, right?"

"Of course. I'll put it on a USB drive for you to take to her," she said to Meghan.

They hadn't solved the mystery of the crooked cop behind Lily's death, but everyone felt a renewed sense of energy and purpose now that they had a plan for how to move forward.

Chapter 43

"I've got so much to tell you," Sarah announced as soon as she walked through Eva's door.

"The rest of us are in the dining room. We were setting up the potluck dishes." They exchanged hellos and everyone fixed themselves a plate before Eva continued. "We'd just been saying we hadn't heard anything new for a few days, but in this case no news is good news doesn't apply. It would have been better if we had, and it was because Lily's killer was caught."

Sarah smacked her forehead.

"Oh, my gosh. I can't believe I didn't tell you that Meghan was arrested two days ago. Well, technically, arrested *three* days ago but I bailed her out two days ago. You would think something like that wouldn't have slipped my mind. In my defense, it's been a little crazy at home and I was spending a lot of time looking for footage on security cams, meeting with Meghan's attorney, and doing my day job. There's so much I have to tell you, so buckle your seatbelts."

After Sarah finished her recital of the events to-date starting with Meghan's arrest, the others were silent. Sarah suppressed a smile. It wasn't really funny because of the nature of the news, and perhaps it was the relief of sharing her worry of the past two days, but seeing their three gobsmacked faces was comical.

"Well, okay, then," Eva broke the silence.

"So, what happens now?" Jennifer asked.

"I don't think there's anything to do but wait for Mike Nicholson to get back to me after he meets with Danielle Larson. Phil and Dennis are still working on identifying the dirty cop, but they haven't made any progress, which is understandable. It's hard to do without raising any suspicions," Sarah said.

"Guess we're back to hurry up and wait. But this time, if you've got any updates, don't keep us in the dark!" Eva's voice was stern, but it didn't reach her eyes, which had a twinkle.

"I promise!" Sarah said. "Cross my heart." She held up her index and middle finger and made a cross over her heart for emphasis.

"In that case, let's clear the dishes and start working on our projects," Eva said.

"I think I'll have mine done by the time we finish tonight," Sarah said. "I can't wait to hang it on our porch!"

The buzzing of four sewing machines soon filled the air.

Chapter 44

"How did it go with your attorney?" Ashley asked when Meghan arrived home from work.

"Great! She was very excited to get the tape. It doesn't help with my drug case but she's going to put in a request for a copy of the surveillance tape through the proper channels in case she needs it later. She's still hoping to find something to prove the drugs were planted. I've got my fingers crossed that Agent Nicholson can get the help he needs from the DA's office, and they can finally make an arrest, so it won't even make it that far."

"Where's Sarah?"

"This is her night for her Cozy Quilts Club meeting. They do a potluck dinner, so it's just the two of us tonight," Ashley replied. "Oh, before I forget, when I came out of my office earlier today, Panda was lying down on the floor in front of the gate. I was able to give him a couple chin scratches and he didn't try to run until Max appeared. That was all it took, and he booked it back to your bedroom."

"I'm afraid that's where he'll stay until this is over," Meghan sighed.

"Have you spoken to Vivian recently?"

"I called her to tell her about being arrested and that I'm staying with you and Sarah, but I haven't spoken to her since. I wanted to wait until we hear back from Agent Nicholson and now that I think about it, it's probably better to not say anything at all until it's over."

"That's probably best. We don't have a lot to share with her anyway and it might upset her to know Sarah found that video of Lily."

Sarah returned later that evening, ready for a show and tell. "Look what I made!" her pride coming through as she held up the spider web house banner she'd made for them to inspect.

"Great job!" Ashley took the banner from Sarah to take a closer look. "Oh, you made a channel for the flagpole to go through, like a curtain does."

"Thankfully, Eva suggested that. I was going to make a hanging sleeve like they do for displaying quilts, but this is so much easier. *Work smarter not, harder, Sarah,*" she said doing a respectable impression of Eva. "I'll put it up tomorrow."

The next morning, Meghan woke up feeling as though there was an elephant on her chest and opened her eyes to find Panda staring back at her. As soon as her eyes opened, he tapped her nose with his paw just in case she hadn't already gotten the message that it was time for breakfast. His, at least.

"Hey, buddy." She scratched his chin with one hand and stretched the other over her head while letting out a big yawn. "If you want me to fix your breakfast, you're going to have to let me get up." She nudged him gently aside so she could get out of bed, and he leaped off to run to the bathroom where she still kept his food dishes and a supply of cat food.

Her stomach growled when the aroma of coffee brewing wafted up the stairs and filled her nostrils. She slipped her phone into the pocket of her robe before moving the gate aside to pass through and put it back in place before walking to the kitchen. Ashley was at the table sipping coffee from a mug and Sarah was at the stove placing strips of bacon in a frying pan. Meghan's stomach growled again as soon as the smell of the bacon reached her, loud enough for everyone to hear.

"Sounds like you're hungry," Sarah teased. "Should I put some in for you?" she asked as she held up a strip of uncooked bacon.

"Yes, please!" she said, with a sheepish smile.

"Help yourself to the coffee," Ashley offered. "I'm going to go take my shower while you two have your breakfast. I've got to get an early start with work this morning."

Meghan poured herself a mugful along with a splash of half and half and sat at the table. As she was about to take a sip, her phone jangled in her pocket nearly causing her to spill the coffee. She frowned as she saw the name on her phone screen.

"It's Mike Nicholson," she explained for Sarah's benefit. "Why would he be calling so early?" she asked rhetorically.

"I've set up a meeting for us with Danielle Larson," he explained after they'd exchanged greetings. "Can you be here at two o'clock this afternoon? She'd also like to have Ms. Pascal here if that can be arranged."

Meghan's shoulders slouched when she heard his request, catching Sarah's attention. She shrugged her shoulders at Meghan and mouthed the words *what's up?*

"I'm putting you on speaker. I'm with Sarah now. Agent Nicholson wants to know if we can meet at Danielle Larson's office this afternoon at two. I'm sorry, but I don't think I can make it. I've already taken a lot of time off from work, and I can't risk getting fired, especially now that I'm going to have to cover the rent by myself until I can find another roommate."

"Would you be able to be there, Ms. Pascal? Danielle has some questions about the recordings Lily made and you might actually be the better person to answer them anyway."

"How long do you think it would take? I have flex hours,

but I can plan my day better if I have some idea ahead of time," Sarah replied.

"I would guess an hour, but I can't guarantee it won't take longer."

Sarah sighed involuntarily, thinking about the time she'd been putting into the case during her usual work hours. Her workload had been light, so it was getting done on time, but it had also taken time away from her evenings to make up the hours.

"Sure, I can be there," she said at last, her voice resigned. "Should I bring copies of the recordings with me?"

"That would be a big help. I'll see you this afternoon."

After Sarah and Mike Nicholson exchanged the address information, Meghan disconnected the call and put the phone back in her pocket. The mood of the room shifted as Meghan sat in stony silence. Even Max felt it and padded over to Meghan, whining softly, and nudged his nose against her hand.

"I'm sorry this is causing so much inconvenience for you. It might be best if Panda and I went back to my apartment, and I'll let my attorney sort this out. I'll pack up our things when I get back from work."

"*Meghan!* Don't be silly. You're not an inconvenience and it isn't safe for you to go back yet," Sarah protested.

"I'm not being *silly*," she insisted, her voice raised, and brushed Max's nose away. Taking the hint, he walked back to his bed and laid down, his muzzle resting on his paws, but his eyes were fixed on Meghan. "I need to get ready for work now, too." Without waiting for Sarah's response, she pushed back in her chair and marched upstairs as Sarah watched, her mouth agape.

"What just happened, Max?"

His ears perked up and he turned in her direction when she addressed him. He uttered a soft whine and laid his head back down on his paws as if to say he had no idea either.

"Did Meghan leave already, Ashley?" Sarah asked when she was showered and ready to start working. Max had bounded over to greet her, his back side now moving in time with his tail, and his tongue washed her hand. "It's so good to see you, too," she said.

Ashley had a puzzled expression on her face. "Yeah. She seemed upset. I asked if she was okay but she told me she didn't want to talk about it. Did something happen after I left?"

"I think I might have made her feel like she was taking too much of my time." Sarah told Ashley about Agent Nicholson's request for Meghan and her to meet with the DA. "I didn't say it would be an inconvenience, but I think she took it that way. Her mood changed immediately. I'm going to go to the meeting at two but I don't know how long it will take. If she comes back before I do, please try to talk her into staying. I don't think she should be at the apartment by herself even though it seems like things have quieted down since she was arrested."

Chapter 45

Sarah was surprised to see Dennis Smith and Phil Roberts in the lobby when she arrived at Danielle Larson's office that afternoon. They looked in her direction, nodding their heads in acknowledgement, and she walked over to join them.

"Are you here about Meghan, too?" she asked.

"Yeah, Mike asked us to come. We're not sure why, though," Phil answered.

Before they could say more, a well-dressed woman in her forties approached them.

"I'm Susan Brown, Ms. Larson's assistant. Would you please follow me?" She didn't wait for their response before turning to walk to a hallway behind the receptionist desk.

Sarah raised her eyebrows as she looked at Phil and Dennis and then followed Susan Brown, with Phil and Dennis tagging along behind to a glass-walled conference room where Mike Nicholson was waiting with a woman she assumed must be Danielle Larson. They declined her offer of a beverage before she opened the door and directed them inside. Mike stood to shake their hands and then introduced Danielle.

"I've told Danielle about Lily's involvement as a CI and her journal and tapes, and what's happened since then with the break-in and the storage locker, so I think she's up to speed, unless there was something I forgot?" Mike asked.

"I have a question," Phil said. "Why are Dennis and I here? Shouldn't Detective Brooks be the one on the case since he's the one assigned to it?"

Danielle and Mike exchanged glances before she continued the conversation.

"Agent Nicholson told me you've been helping Meghan Doherty and Ms. Pascal," she said turning to Sarah. "I've had some experience with Detective Brooks and I don't like to speak ill of someone in front of others, especially co-workers, but I have a lack of confidence having him read into what we have planned. Your records are exemplary, and Agent Nicholson has vouched for your ability to maintain confidentiality." She paused as though to weigh her words before continuing. "Lily Sullivan wasn't wrong about there being a crooked cop involved. We've been investigating that angle for some time now but didn't have enough evidence to make an arrest or for that matter, *who* we should arrest. We still don't, but we're hoping Lily's recordings will provide us with a clue as to his identity. Mike, do you have the copies of her recordings, and the video from the day Ms. Sullivan was killed?"

"I don't. I had a meeting that took longer than expected so I wasn't able to go back to my office and make it here on time. I asked Sarah if she would make another copy for you."

"Do you have those, Ms. Pascal?"

"Yes, I put them on a USB drive." She reached into her purse and handed the drive to Danielle, who plugged it into the laptop on the conference table.

"It would probably be easier if I let you do this," Danielle told Sarah.

After making several selections, she displayed it on a screen where they could all see the video. When they finished, she queued up the list of recordings and chose the one Lily had labeled Randy and his boss and matched the date of the surveillance tape. They were listening to the exchange between Lily and Randy when they heard the voice of the unidentified man and Phil suddenly sat up at attention.

"I recognize that voice!"

All eyes turned his way.

"That's Adam Parker from the Bangor International division,"

"Would you play that back, please?" Dennis asked.

Sarah queued it up and played it again.

"I would never have seen that one coming, but you're right!" Dennis agreed after hearing it the second time.

Sarah had been quiet, but her curiosity got the better of her. "Now, what do you do about it?"

Chapter 46

"We'll need to get Internal Affairs involved but I want to time it so we don't jeopardize the drug case. Do you have any idea who the mole is at the DEA?" Danielle asked Mike.

"I'm still working on that. Whoever hacked into my computer did a good job of covering their tracks."

"Maybe I can help."

Danielle turned to Sarah. "How?"

"My day job is in cyber security. If I had permission and Mike's log-in information, I could see if there's anything his IT person missed. I would need something official authorizing that, though. I'm not going to go poking around on just a verbal okay. There's no way I'll put my job and career on the line."

"I'll work on that," Danielle told her.

"Have you got enough to pick up Randy Hughes so you could bring him in for questioning?" Phil asked Mike.

"I might be able to bring him in on a drug charge, but there's nothing to tie him to Lily Sullivan's murder."

"We have the bugs that they placed in their apartment…" Sarah was about to add *right after Lily was killed* but caught herself. Sarah frantically searched her memory of who she'd told and what she'd said so she wouldn't expose herself. She felt Dennis and Phil looking at her and glanced over. There was a *what the heck* look in their eyes and she realized it wasn't just Danielle and Mike who didn't already know about them.

"Wait, back up. Lily Sullivan's apartment was bugged?" Danielle asked.

"I'm sorry, I forgot none of you knew about that. Yes, that's how we assumed they found out about the envelope and that it was in the apartment." She didn't notice any change in Danielle's expression, so quickly went on. "I had the guy who removed them keep them in case we needed them. This seems like the time to turn them over. I don't know if they'll have any fingerprints on them but even if they don't, maybe there would be another way to connect them. Maybe proof they bought them?" Sarah suggested.

"It wouldn't hurt to have them in our custody, but we need to make sure we have a proper chain of evidence. Was it documented with photos to identity the locations where they were found?" Danielle asked.

"Yes, Hank was very careful to make sure he did that and to take a photo of the serial numbers at the same time so they would match the scene."

"Did he wear gloves?"

"Yes, and Meghan and Vivian didn't know where they'd been placed until Hank came to remove them so their prints shouldn't be on them either."

"It might be a problem that there has been so much time between when they were removed and when they're turned over to us, but we'll deal with that," Danielle said. "Please have him get in touch with my office and we'll arrange to take possession of them and take his statement."

"I'll do that as soon as I get home."

There was a moment of silence in the room and then Sarah let out an exasperated sigh and rolled her eyes as she had an epiphany. "Dawn breaks over Marblehead. I was so focused on finding an alibi for Meghan that it never occurred to me until now to find a security camera that would have captured Randy Hughes and the other guy… Adam Parker… entering and leaving her apartment complex. If they were with Lily earlier that day, it makes sense to me that they could be the ones responsible for her death," she added hoping to keep up the ruse that she didn't already know that for a fact. "I knew there weren't any security cameras for the building and didn't follow up. I'll see what else is close enough and the right angle to catch them." She rubbed her finger absentmindedly back and forth across her chin. "I should probably check the streets nearby. They could have parked their car somewhere else and walked over," she said, more to herself than the others. "I'll need to see a photo of Parker's face to make sure it's him. We only have a picture of his back to the camera in the video."

"I can get one for you," Phil offered.

"That's a great idea. If you can find anything, that would prove they were in the area during the time Lily died. I can work with that to press him about her," Mike said.

"Wouldn't he wonder why you're asking about who killed Lily if you're DEA?" Sarah asked.

"She was his CI," Phil explained.

"Oh, right. I get it now."

"I think that's all we need from you for now, Ms. Pascal, so you're free to go," Danielle said. "I'd like you to stay, detectives. I'll need more information about Adam Parker."

Sarah stood to leave. "I'll start looking for any proof Hughes and Parker were in the area and get back to you if I find anything. *When* I find anything," Sarah said more assertively. She was determined to do that no matter how long it took her. The heaviness that had been Sarah's constant shadow since she found out about Lily's murder lifted. *We might finally be getting somewhere.* In her excitement to get back to start the search, she nearly broke into a run as she left the room and forced herself to slow down. *Finally, I've got new leads to track down.*

She hadn't gone far when she heard Phil calling for her to wait up. She turned and her stomach turned to butterflies when she saw the scowl on his face.

"What was that about the bugs? Why didn't you tell us?"

"I'm sorry you found out that way. We had talked about telling you earlier, but we were afraid it could get you in trouble." She continued to explain the reasons she'd discussed earlier with the quilt club.

He stopped scowling and nodded his head slowly as he absorbed her explanation.

"Okay, I get it now and you were probably right not to say anything. I'll tell Dennis once we're out of the meeting. I should get back now. I made an excuse to use the men's room so I could catch up to you."

"Still friends?" Sarah asked, a half-smile on her face.

"Still friends," he replied, returning her smile, and turned to walk back to Danielle's office.

Sarah cocked her head down slightly and her eyebrows raised as she let out her breath. *Phew!* The last thing she wanted was to make an enemy of Phil and Dennis. She turned to leave once again, with not quite as much bounce in her step, but still feeling the sense of excitement that the case would be resolved soon.

Chapter 47

"Did something happen at the meeting that has you worried?"

"No, but my spidey senses are tingling."

"Should I start calling you Annalise?" Ashley teased.

"No, but it might not be a bad idea for me to talk to her. She could tap in to see if she has the same feeling. I'll do that after dinner. I've also got more investigating to do with security cameras. It might take me a few hours."

"I have some paperwork to catch up on myself. Sounds like we've got a fun night ahead."

Ninety minutes later, Sarah's disappointment threatened to destroy her earlier optimism. Her search for footage of the apartment building grounds and entrances turned up empty. She sighed. *Don't give up yet.* She rolled her shoulders and moved her head in a circle hearing an audible crack. She widened the search to cameras capturing views of the streets surrounding the building. Two streets away from the apartment building she spotted a car that looked familiar. Zooming in, she knew it was the same one driven by Randy Hughes. The time stamp was within fifteen minutes of Meghan's return to the apartment. She advanced the footage slowly. *Gotcha!* She fist-pumped to put an exclamation on her discovery. Randy Hughes and Adam Parker, if Phil was right, appeared on her screen and walked to the car. Just before getting in, Parker faced the camera as he scanned the street. *I bet you thought no one saw you, didn't you? Guess what? You were wrong!*

She'd been so busy looking at the footage, she hadn't checked her texts or emails to see if Phil had sent her the picture of Adam Parker. Scrolling through her emails, she found what she was looking for and opened the attachment. A smug smile crossed Sarah's face.

Chapter 48

Come on, Meghan, pick up! It was Sarah's third attempt and each time the call had gone to voice mail. Texting instead that they'd had a break in the case, she hit the Send arrow and hoped for the best. *I know you can be stubborn, Meg, but come on. We need to talk.*

Who do I call? Phil? Dennis? Or Mike? Decision made; she stabbed the screen.

"Phillip Roberts."

A sense of relief washed over her when she heard his voice. *At least somebody is answering their phone.*

"Phil, it's Sarah Pascal. I hope I'm not calling you too late, but I found what we were looking for!"

"No kidding? That's great! Have you told Dennis or Mike yet?"

"I thought you and Dennis were the better ones to tell. The photo you sent me of Adam Parker matches the new footage I found of him with Randy Hughes. You're the lucky one to hear the news first because R comes before S."

"And here I was feeling flattered that you called me first."

Sarah felt his smile coming through the phone.

"Well, I guess you should get the credit since you're the one who sent me the photo," she conceded.

"I'll call Dennis as soon as we get off the phone. Will you be home tomorrow morning? We could drop by so you can show us the footage. I don't think I'm wrong about his voice, but if the face matches, it's case closed. At least for phase one."

"Absolutely! Should I tell Mike or Danielle Larson?"

Phil hesitated. "Let's wait until you show us the tape. If it's not him, we're back to square one about who Randy Hughes's partner is. Make a copy of the video anyway. We'll need it one way or the other."

Sarah was shutting down her computer for the night when her phone rang. *Finally!*

"Meghan, I've been so worried about you!"

"I'm sorry. I needed some time. When I told Vivian what happened, she told me I was getting my feelings hurt over nothing and I should call you. So… here I am."

"I'm sorry, too. It came out wrong. No, wait. I'm not being completely honest. I *was* thinking about how much time I've taken during my usual work hours the past couple weeks. Sometimes I can be hyper responsible and feel guilty if I'm not at my desk from nine to five. When it comes down to it, though, I really do have flex hours and as long as my work is getting done on time, it doesn't matter what those hours are. I hope you didn't think I don't want to help."

"I did feel that way then. But I don't now. I can't tell you how much I appreciate all you've done for me."

"You'd do the same for me. *Welll,* maybe not *everything* the same."

Sarah's chest expanded as the tension she'd been holding released.

"Drop by after you get off work tomorrow. I've got a lot to tell you."

Chapter 49

Phil and Dennis peered over Sarah's shoulder watching her monitor. She zoomed in when Adam Parker appeared on the footage.

"That's definitely him," Phil said.

"Yup," Dennis affirmed.

"If you could make a copy…" Dennis began.

"Already done." She handed him a USB drive. "Should I have made one for Mike and Danielle, too?"

"No, I'll take this one to Danielle," he said as he put it into an evidence bag and labeled it. "I'll let her decide what to do about giving a copy to Mike. It should be enough for him to just watch it, so he'll be able to recognize Adam Parker."

"Now that we have this and the footage you made earlier at the waterfront with Lily, it's going to be a lot harder for him to deny he's involved. Your help has been invaluable," Phil acknowledged.

"Meghan is my friend, Phil. There's nothing I wouldn't do to help her."

"Just keep it legal." He winked, but Sarah knew he was only half-kidding.

"How is this going to play out with Brooks?" she asked.

Phil and Dennis exchanged looks. Phil shrugged.

"We'll worry about that tomorrow, Scarlett."

Chapter 50

Sarah's email notification buzzed. Her pulse quickened when she read the name **Danielle Larson**. Her eyes skimmed through the text of the message and then opened the attachment. *Hallelujah!* It was the written consent for her to access Mike Nicholson's computer. If she was lucky, it could give them the last piece of the puzzle about who was working behind the scenes. She debated with the angel on her left shoulder to *do it now* but the angel on her right shoulder and her sense of responsibility won. She resumed working on her current project. It took an hour of excruciating patience and concentration, but she did it.

Once she was in the system, Sarah typed in the username and password Mike had given her at their meeting with Danielle. There was no evidence of the usual programs like keystroke tracking, but she hadn't expected it. *Mike said you were good. He wasn't kidding.* Thirty minutes later and she still had no clue who was responsible or how they'd gotten in. She scrunched her eyebrows and her lips flattened into a single line. She liked a good challenge, but this one was kicking her butt.

Ashley softly walked a few steps into the room but recognized the look on Sarah's face and knew this wasn't the time to interrupt her for dinner. She'd try again in an hour if Sarah still hadn't come downstairs. Max stood in the doorway and watched Sarah after Ashley left. Even he knew she was in the zone. Sarah might not be ready for dinner, but he was. He turned tail and trotted down to the kitchen.

There you are! She smiled smugly. *Thought you could outsmart everyone, didn't you? You didn't count on having Sarah Pascal tracking you down.*

Sarah stretched her arms above her head and laced her hands together as she leaned to one side and then the other. Her stomach growled and she was shocked to see what time it was. *Darn! I missed dinner.* She inhaled as the aroma of roasted chicken broke through her work fog, filling her nose with its promise of deliciousness, and once again her stomach complained loudly.

"I'm sorry. I lost all track of time. Is that for me?"

"It is. I was about to put it in the fridge. It probably would have tasted better hot, but it shouldn't take long to reheat." She covered the plate with plastic wrap and put it in the microwave.

"You look pleased with yourself. Does that mean you figured it out, whatever *it* was?"

"I did, indeed."

Chapter 51

"I've got a lead on a drug deal with Randy Hughes. We're setting up a surveillance and with luck we'll be able to arrest him tonight." Mike Nicholson was in Sarah's kitchen. "I didn't want to take any chances the mole in our department would find out," he explained, when he saw the *what are you doing here?* look on Sarah's face.

"I'm glad you're here. It saves me getting in touch with you. I figured out who your mole is."

His eyebrows shot up. "Really? Who is it?"

"Does the name Jack Smith mean anything to you?"

"Yeah. He's one of our IT guys."

"Did he claim your computer needed some upgrades and he'd do it while you were on vacation?"

His face registered his understanding. "As a matter of fact, he did. That's when he did it, isn't it? And there was no reason to suspect him because that's his job."

"I did some background checking on him. He's in over his head financially but he deposited five thousand dollars in his bank account right about that time. My guess is either Randy Hughes or Adam Parker offered him a way out and this was what they traded the money for."

"I'll get in touch with Danielle. She'll need to know how you traced it back to him. I'm sure she'll be in touch directly. There are a lot of balls in the air right now. We're hoping we can persuade Hughes to flip on Parker without tipping him off. You shouldn't discuss this with Phil Roberts or Dennis Smith either. We don't want any slip ups and they're in more than they should be already."

Sarah nodded. "I understand. Good luck tonight!"

"Thanks. I'll let you know how it goes as soon as I can."

Sarah leaned against the door after she closed it behind Mike. "We're getting closer, Lily," she said softly. Invisible arms wrapped Sarah in an embrace, and she smiled.

Chapter 52

Randy Hughes was sticking to his story that he had no idea who Lily Sullivan was.

"We've got video of you with her, Randy. You and your boss, Adam Parker."

Mike saw the pupils dilate in Randy's eyes, giving him away, but he quickly resumed his poker face.

"I don't know any Lily Sullivan or Adam Parker. You've got the wrong guy. It's not me."

Mike pulled the photo of Randy, Adam, and Lily out of the folder he'd placed on the table and slid it across to Randy. "You're telling me that's not you?"

Randy barely looked at the photo before meeting Mike's eyes. "I must have one of those faces. This guy just looks like me."

"And I suppose if we do a voice comparison, this guy's voice won't match yours either?" Mike played one of Lily's recordings of her and Randy discussing a deal.

"That b…" he snarled and stopped.

"We've got you, Randy, but that's not the worst of it. We know you killed Lily and you've been trying to frame her roommate. You're the one who planted the drugs in her trunk, aren't you?"

They stared each other down and Randy's stony expression didn't waver.

"We've got proof you were in her apartment. We searched your storage unit and before you try to complain, we had a warrant. If you didn't know her, how is that we found an envelope belonging to her in your file cabinet?"

No response. The silence in the room stretched out as the two men played their cat and mouse game.

"The prosecutor's office is ready to file first degree homicide charges against you, Randy."

Mike noticed Randy's left eye twitch. *You've got his attention.*

"Maybe it was an accident. Maybe your boss made you do it. Tell us what happened and who he is, and the DA might agree to reduce the charge to involuntary manslaughter. Of course, I can't authorize that, but I've got a good feeling we can work out a deal. You and I both know you're low man on the totem pole and it's your boss who's the big prize. What do you say, Randy? First degree homicide or involuntary manslaughter?"

"I say I want my lawyer."

Those were the dreaded words Mike didn't want to hear. His heart sank but there was nothing else he could do now. *I blew it.*

Chapter 53

Max leaped up from his bed and raced downstairs, startling Sarah. She wasn't expecting anyone, but it sounded like Max's barks were coming from the front door. They didn't have the urgency of his *I'm here to protect you from this stranger at our door* tone, but Ashley wasn't at home to check it out. She held her breath as she listened, hoping it was a false alarm, but the barks were joined by knocks. *Darn, not his imagination.* Sighing, she pulled herself away from her work and went to investigate.

The sheer curtain covering the window in the door partially obscured their details, but Sarah recognized Meghan and Mike standing there.

"It's okay, Max. They're friends."

Woof!

She didn't need Eva to interpret that he understood.

She could feel their excitement as soon as she opened the door. Meghan was bouncing as she walked past Sarah, and she hadn't ever seen Mike smile the way he was smiling now.

Meghan perched on the edge of the couch; her hands clasped in her lap. "You can tell her," she said to Mike and then looked back at Sarah. Her body language shouted we've got something exciting to share.

"Randy Hughes made a deal. I thought for sure he was going to lawyer up but once Danielle explained the situation, he agreed. There was some bargaining, but they hammered out a plea deal once she agreed to reduce the charges if he would wear a wire and get Adam Parker to confess to his involvement both with Lily and the drug ring. He got the confession last night. I don't think this would have happened so fast if all of you hadn't been involved. Between the video footage and finding Lily's envelope in the storage unit, it was enough to tip Randy over the edge and his attorney convinced him the plea deal was better than claiming he wasn't involved and going to trial."

Sarah broke into a wide grin. "That's fantastic! Has anyone been in touch with Vivian?"

"I called her the first thing this morning after Adam Parker was arrested," Mike said.

"It must be bittersweet for her. Lily helped bring down the drug ring but if I'm understanding this right, no one is going to pay for Lily's death." Sarah said.

Meghan's face clouded and there was sadness in her eyes. "Yeah. It helps a little knowing that it really was an accident. Randy told them the same…" she caught herself before slipping about Lily's account of the night of her death. She'd forgotten for a moment that Mike wasn't a party to that and there was no way to tell him about Sarah's communication with Lily. "Randy told them Lily stumbled while they were struggling and fell backwards into the counter. He claimed she didn't have a pulse and that, along with not having a reason to be there, is why he didn't call 911."

They were all quiet for a moment before Sarah's face lit up. "We need to have a celebration with the others."

"That's a great idea!" Meghan agreed.

I CAN'T BELIEVE *everyone is able to come on such short notice* Sarah thought after arranging for the Club ladies, Meghan, Mike, Phil, and Dennis to meet at her house that evening. Vivian wouldn't be able to be there in person, but they'd arranged to FaceTime with her.

Mike was the last to arrive and held up a bottle when Sarah opened the door.

"I thought an occasion like this called for champagne."

Sarah smiled. "I couldn't agree more. Follow me. Everyone is in the dining room. I only told them the Cliff notes version. I thought they should hear the rest from you and Meghan."

After introductions were made, Mike and Meghan recounted what they had shared with Sarah earlier that day.

"And even better, Randy Hughes confessed to planting the drugs in my trunk. I've been cleared of all charges!"

"Did you hear from Detective Brooks?" Sarah asked.

Meghan snorted. "Like that's going to happen. I don't think his ego could handle admitting to my face that he was wrong about me."

"What happened with the IT guy who leaked the information that Lily was your confidential informant?" Jennifer asked Mike.

"He was arrested, too. His story is that it started out like it did for Lily. He needed money and he thought he could make it a one-time bribe when they set up the deal. You see where this is going. They told him if he didn't continue as their mole, they would hurt his wife. They'll probably work something out since he's agreed to testify against Adam Parker."

"Did you find out if it was someone at the police station who was helping Parker?" Annalise asked Phil and Dennis.

"Internal Affairs did. After Danielle Larson got them involved, they were able to figure it out. And Parker was only too happy to give him up when he thought it might help his case," Dennis told them.

"Was that the same person who tipped Randy Hughes off about the graveside service?" Jennifer asked.

"No. It was Parker's secretary. It was just like you figured that she called the funeral home and made up a story to get the information. She claimed to be Lyndon Brooks's secretary so it wouldn't come back on Parker if anyone followed up. He was able to con her into doing it because they were having an affair. He'll probably need a divorce lawyer along with a defense attorney," Phil said, chuckling.

"Should we break out the champagne?" Mike asked.

"Absolutely. Go ahead and fill the glasses but wait until I can FaceTime Vivian before we make a toast." Sarah set up her iPad and Vivian appeared on the screen. "We're just about to celebrate but we didn't want to do it without you. Everybody scooch in so Vivian can see us." All nine of them clustered together. "Okay, ready? To Lily!"

Everyone raised their glasses and repeated the toast as Vivian smiled through her tears.

Meghan was the last to leave.

"I couldn't have made it through this without you," she said as she wrapped Sarah in her arms.

"You know I'll always be there for you."

They clung to each other; all that had happened strengthening the bond they shared.

Chapter 54

"Aren't they pretty?" Eva pinned the last banner to the design wall she'd set up earlier in the day to display them.

Annalise patted Sarah on the back. "You really upped your game with this project, Sarah."

Sarah's face flushed a light pink but for once, she didn't deflect the compliment.

"It was a great idea to hang them on your design wall so we can admire them side by side, Eva," Jennifer said. "I can't wait to hang mine on my house."

"When I was taking mine down this afternoon so I could bring it tonight, my neighbor happened to be outside and told me how much she liked it and that I should leave it up. She thought I was taking it down for good and was happy to hear I was only taking it down to bring here," Sarah told them, her face beaming with pride. "Oh, before I forget, Meghan and Vivian asked me to thank all of you again for your part in solving the mystery of how Lily died and clearing Meghan's name."

"It's what we do now, isn't it?" Annalise gave Sarah a wink.

Watch out Jessica Fletcher. The Cozy Quilts Club is taking over.

Eva translated Reuben's jibe.

"On that note, raise your glasses, ladies." She waited until the others held their drinks up to toast. "To our next project, be it a quilt, a mystery, or both!"

Three voices joined her in a chorus of "Hear! Hear!"

Also by Marsha DeFilippo

Arizona Dreams

Deja vu Dreams

Disillusioned Dreams

A Cozy Quilts Club Mystery series

Follow the Crumbs

Finding the Treasure

Summer's End

Counting Coins

Pulling Out the Hidden Stitches

(Download the story by typing

https://dl.bookfunnel.com/15vlqk2g9h

in your choice of a browser window or use the QR code below.)

About the Author

After retiring from her day job of nearly 33 years, Marsha DeFilippo has embarked on a new career of writing books. She is also a quilter and lifelong avid crafter who has yet to try a craft she doesn't like. She spends her winters in Arizona and the remainder of the year in Maine.

**For more information, please visit my website:
marsha defilippo.com**

To get the latest information on new releases, excerpts and more, be sure to sign up for Marsha's newsletter.
https://marshadefilippo.com/newsletter

Made in the USA
Monee, IL
20 January 2025

10290963R00109